The Kind of Light
That Shines
on Texas

/ / / / / /

Also by Reginald McKnight

Moustapha's Eclipse

I Get on the Bus

Living Writers is a course and readings series offered annually at Colgate University. Students are directed in the study mainly of important works of contemporary fiction, although poetry and nonfictional prose are represented in the program. After extensive research, students interview the author of the work they have studied and attend a reading of new work. Their object is to learn the various ways in which, according to the artists, literary art is made. Among the guests of the course during its fifteen years in the curriculum: Alfred Kazin, James Laughlin, David Bradley, John McGahern, William Kennedy, Paula Fox, Cynthia Ozick, Paule Marshall, James Alan McPherson, Grace Paley, Reynolds Price, Caryl Philips, Bharati Mukherjee, and, of course, Reginald McKnight. The course is designed to consider the cultural forces expressed in the publication of serious writing. The appearance of this edition of Mr. McKnight's collection suggests the interest in and commitment to living literature at Colgate.

The Kind of Light That Shines on Texas

/ / / / / /

Stories by
Reginald McKnight

Published in cooperation with
the Living Writers course at
Colgate University

SOUTHERN METHODIST
UNIVERSITY PRESS
Dallas

The characters and events in this book are fictitious. Any similarity to real persons, living or dead, is coincidental and not intended by the author.

Requests for permission to reproduce material from this work should be sent to:
    Rights and Permissions
    Southern Methodist University Press
    PO Box 750415
    Dallas, Texas 75275-0415

Some of the stories in this collection were first published in the following publications: "The Homunculus" in *Colorado College Magazine*; "Quitting Smoking" in *The Kenyon Review*; "The Kind of Light That Shines on Texas" in *The Kenyon Review* and *Prize Stories 1990: The O. Henry Awards* (Doubleday, 1990); and "Roscoe in Hell" in *Black American Literature Forum*.

LIBRARY OF CONGRESS CATALOGING-IN-PUBLICATION DATA

McKnight, Reginald, 1956–
    The kind of light that shines on Texas : stories / by Reginald McKnight. — 1st Southern Methodist University Press ed.
        p.   cm.
    "Published in cooperation with the Living writers course at Colgate University."
    ISBN 0-87074-414-3 (pbk. : acid-free paper)
    1. Afro-Americans—Social life and customs—Fiction. I. Title.
[PS3563.C3833K56 1996]
813'.54—dc20   96-9063

Printed in the United States of America on acid-free paper

10 9 8 7 6 5 4 3 2 1

For Frank and Pearl McKnight

Contents

/ / / / / /

My sincerest thanks go to the following people for their advice and encouragement: James Yaffe, Michele McKnight, David Mason, Tom Clark, Gideon Yaffe, Hilary Masters, Ingrid Mundari, Trudy Palmer, Keith A. Owens, Kit Ward, and Barbara Schoichet.

The Kind of Light
That Shines
on Texas

/ / / / / /

The Homunculus:
A Novel in
One Chapter

/ / / / / /

Many, many years ago there lived a young artist, who, the people said, was full of great potential and great talent. What kind of artist was he? you ask, knowing full well that in our present age almost anyone from a computer programmer to an oil twiller to a grocery boxer is called an artist. Well, my friend, this young man was skilled in many, many things. First of all, he was a marvelous poet. Some say his poetry was on par with the finest, most well known poets of that day, though the young man was barely into his twenties when his third book of poetry was published.

He was an adept fiction writer, too. His short stories and novels were the talk of the entire Realm. His saddest stories could squeeze the heart like a great fist. The funniest could rattle the ribs and stop the breath. He wrote with a spare style that somehow cast arabesque shadows in the mind, causing his reading audience to ponder the depths of the soul in all its turns and bends.

It is well known even in our present age that he could sculpt and paint in such a wide array of moods, styles, themes, and patterns that he held the entire art world breathlessly wondering in what untrodden ground he would next place his intrepid, daring feet.

It is also said that he could sing and play lyre, lute, kleetello, guitar, dulcimer, fiddle, cello, and vibraphone. His voice rang with such power and clarity that his audiences (particularly the females) were said to be held in a sort of speechless rapture for days and days after one of his concerts.

He was also very handsome, kind, modest, soft-spoken, gentle, and honest. He respected his elders, was generous to his peers, fatherly to the young. He gave alms to the poor, cheer to the sullen, wisdom to the foolish, attention to the marginal.

But he was not happy.

You ask, my friend, why this wonderful soul, this light of the world, this one, who, as our people say, so clearly showed the "thumbprint of the Old One" was not happy? No one knew. Not even the young artist himself really knew, or at least he was unwilling to say. Those of a spiritual inclination said that it was his karma. That he was born an artistic genius on a plane in which he could neither quite fully express himself nor be completely understood. Those of a more skeptical persuasion — there were a handful — said that it was because of a deeply embedded but well-hidden vanity, and a lust for absolute power. They said that all he created, either consciously or unconsciously, he created to subjugate the minds and hearts of his audience and ultimately to make them his slaves.

But others said — though none had ever heard him confess this — that it was because he could not have the love of one woman: Nohla, the beautiful daughter of the kindly, humble miller, Rafkhan. They said that the two were in love for only one year, though in secret (Rafkhan had great hopes that Nohla would one day become a surgeon, and he would sooner lose his right hand than see his child's future fuddled by love), but then, quite suddenly, Nohla, either because she saw something in the young artist that was akin to what his detractors, those few skeptics, saw, or because she became convinced her father was right, ended the affair. All that we can say is that she carried some deep, unfathomable discomfiture in her bosom that told her she could no longer be with this man, and so she shattered his young heart.

Whatever the reasons, the young man stopped creating and entertaining before the year was over. He seldom left his home after a while, but sat inside for weeks and months on end, brooding and pacing. He let his beard grow long, let his countenance sour, and ate little. It has been said that his servants heard him sing from time to time, but only to himself, almost in a whisper, in a cracked, atonal voice. He admitted very few friends: his brother, Rhoe the Mighty, still, statistically, the greatest treadleback in the history of our national sport, and his close friend and neighbor, Azzizan. Neither Rhoe nor Azzizan could bear to see their young loved one in such pain and grief. But when they would ask him, "What ails ye, brother?" "What grinds thee, friend?," all that he is said to have answered was, "Me? I'm just thinking. Just thinking, that's all." Then one day, after an evening of putting mouth to ear and ear to mouth in an alehouse not far from the young artist's house, Rhoe and Azzizan decided they should persuade the young man to take a journey. After several weeks they succeeded.

The young artist took only a fortnight preparing for the journey, traveling throughout the Greater Realm to say good-bye to all his friends and patrons. Then, at last, he set sail for what legend calls the Land of Light and Dark. He was at sea for some three months, and during the entire journey kept himself in his cabin in much the same way he had kept to himself in his home. It was a journey without incident, for the most part. The crew on the ship were of the usual rambunctious sort, and often kept the young man awake nights with their perpetual revelry, pranks, and boisterous, bold talk about what they would do once putting down in the Land of Light and Dark.

The Land, as you know, is no more. It was swallowed by our oceans uncountable years ago. Our archaeologists have recovered, what? a few buttons, a chalice or two, a bronze slingshot? We know so little of the physical place. All we have are these stories, and who knows precisely how true they are. The Land is now a place more of mystery and legend than of history and fact. In it, we are told, were five of the eight known mysteries of the Ur-Realm. It was known to be a land of both blood-freezing violence and beauty so profound that it is said the Old One actually slept there. With its winged people with the skin of polished obsidian who spoke only in proverbs, its diamond white rivers that cut through soil so rich that the meanest, bitterest seed would sprout into waxy green leaves and pulpy fruit, with its dramatic waterfalls, its infinite canyons, its smoke blue mountains, its caverns of gold and jade, its many curiously constructed beasts, who, it is said spoke the language of the winged people, the young artist told himself that no other land could bring out in him what had been so deeply buried.

The first several months in this strange land went well for the young artist. He made many friends, ate strange and delightful foods, swam the diamond waters, drank sweet teas that made him dream of Nohla. He shaved off his beard and dressed in the fine, bright clothing of the obsidian people. He learned some of their language, which inspired in him sage thought. He let them carry him aloft and show him the world as only birds could see it. Things went well for him. His heart grew big again. And one morning he awoke in a creative flame. He began to write!

It had been so long since he had written anything that he took the cautious road and began keeping a

journal. In it he wrote of everything he was seeing and
doing and feeling. He devoted just as much time to
describing, in detail, all the strange fruits and vegetables there as he did to describing the people and the
geography. He also wrote of the things in his heart, of
his dissatisfaction with his past work, his weaknesses as
a human being, and his great love for Nohla.

His writing, steady, furious, impassioned, came to
take up more and more of his time. He seldom ventured
outside his house, and he spent less and less time with
his friends. And on three occasions his friend N'Tho, a
good man, a tall, intelligent man who'd saved him from
the grip of a waterfall he'd ventured too close to in his
first week in the country, rapped on his door and asked
him, would he not care for a slice of yellow sunshine, a
bowl of friendship, and a cup of laughter. And each
time the young artist would smile and thank him, but
say no. "Your land has . . . has, uh, set me afire, and the
smithy's best work is at noon." And N'Tho would turn
and leave, saying, "Is it true that when the bird finishes
its nest it no longer cares whether the grass grows?"

"No, no, good friend," would be the reply, "but the,
uh, whispers of the heart are greater than the screams of
the flesh." And one, two, three times did he close the
door on the retreating back of N'Tho.

It wasn't long before he was virtually friendless, before, as we say in the southern region, his kitchen grew
quiet. But he never noticed. His work had reached such
a feverish intensity that not even he realized for the

longest time that his journal had become first a novel, then a poem, then a prayer, then a chant, then a one-act play, an opera — it actually made sound! — a painting, a sculpture — and then — wonder of wonders — the thing became flesh! A miniature version of himself!

Of course, finally he did notice himself, but it did take a while, for his work still compelled him, devoured him, you might say, and — quite naturally — his mind was rather distracted. But one day as he scribbled and chiseled and stitched upon the . . . text . . . we shall call it, he began to notice that his fingers were clutching his own throat, in a manner of speaking, and his thumbs were shaping his own, well . . . it wasn't a sentence anymore, he had to admit to himself. It wasn't a canvas or clay, it was — "My chin!" he said aloud. "Blessed Old One, I —"

" 'Bout time you noticed, homes."

"You're me —"

"Uh-huh —"

"A little version of —"

" 'At's right."

"Oh my."

He silently disrobed, put out his candle, and went to sleep. When he awoke the next morning, his mind felt clear, and he chuckled, thinking to himself that perhaps he had been working too hard. He decided to get up, wash, have a large breakfast, and spend the day visiting his friends. But as he reached for his robes he saw his little self sitting on the edge of his writing desk, eating a page of his journal. "What are you doing?" he demanded.

The homunculus shot his black beady gaze at his maker. "You mean what am *I* doing?" he said.

"Who are you? What are you? Where did you come —"

"What it look like I'm doing, fool?"

"That's my journal! Stop that, you —"

"But I'ma tell you something, brother. You got to cut down on the salt. See, when you bending over your work, hacking away like you do, you be sweating all *over* these pages. But other than that they pretty good." The young artist looked at the little creature, and he could not help but be torn between a number of emotions: anger, fear, astonishment, and, perhaps most discomforting of all, admiration, for the little man was perfect in every way that the eyes could discern. Black eyes and black hair, white teeth, sharp jawbones, powerful arms, long fingers, seamless skin, a spine as straight as a shaft of light. He was magnificent, and were it not for the little man's crude language, and most especially, were it not for the fact that the little one was eating his journal by the fistful, the artist would have liked to sit the chap on his knee and study him. But the very fact that the homunculus *was* eating his journal kept all action at bay, impelled the cycle of these emotions.

Finally, however, as the little man reached for the third of the eight-hundred-eighty-eight-page manuscript, the young artist possessed himself enough to clutch the finger-sized arm of this literary gourmand. "Do you mind?" the young man said.

The homunculus looked him up and down. He arched an eyebrow. "Yes I do, man. Lemme go."

"You're making a mess of my journal."

"Well I ad*mit* I ain't got good table manners, but I'ma still eat this thing."

"Like Hatsax you will!" And the young artist grabbed the pitcher near his bed and smashed it down where the homunculus stood. But as you might guess, it was in vain, for the creature had disappeared.

The young artist spent the better part of the day overturning his rooms in search of the creature's hole or portal or whatever it might be the thing had come through. He ordered his servants to keep the place clean and to make sure that the doors remained shut and that the window screens were kept in place. Nevertheless, he found nothing. Exhausted, stiff with anger, he gathered himself enough to brew a cup of tea and sit down to write. He wanted to rewrite those first two pages of his journal. But this was a problem because the last several months of work had flown with such momentum that there had simply been no time for him to stop and reread what he'd written. He'd no idea where to begin. "I remember something about fruits and vegetables . . . and people, yes, people with wings, and Nora, my love." Nora? he thought. No, it was Noah, or Nova, or . . . Really he was not sure, and it occurred to him that he was too long out of touch with those things that had moved him, lo those months ago, to journey to this land and rediscover his creative embers. "Yes," he said, "first thing tomorrow I will visit my old friends the What's-Their-Names and that nice tall fellow whose life I saved when he ventured too close to the falls, and I'll see those people and talk to them or something. Perhaps they can explain this nonsense." He drank one last cup of tea and went to bed.

A warm yellow light leaked into his bedroom and crept up his sheets. He opened his eyes, then aimed his hearing at what he'd dreamed was the sound of frying fish. He sniffed the air, half expecting his nose to fill with the sweet smell of ocean pod or peacefish or tinshells. But he could smell nothing. And the frying sound, he discovered, was not the sound of fresh fish bubbling in hot oil but the sound of crackling paper. "It's back," he hissed.

The little artist licked a finger, then licked another. "Morning, blood. Thought you wasn't never gonna get up."

The young artist hurled the sheet off his legs and sprang to his feet. "What are you doing to me?"

"Is you stupid? Take a scope at y'self, boy. I'm here 'cause you here. But yo, what kinda ink you use on page eight, homely? It's giving me serious gastronomics."

As though he were alone, the young man snapped his fingers, and said, "It's the tea! Of course, the tea!

Oh, Blessed the Old One be! That's it, yes, that's it and I swear it off forever." He snatched up his clothes and dressed himself on the way out of the room, thinking these thoughts: "What I do first, you see, is go see my friends and have them over to my place. If they see no Little Me — and they won't — I'll know for certain that it was the tea I've been drinking, not to mention the strain of working, the poor diet, the dearth of sunshine and exercise and fresh air. Oh my dear friends, oh my dear Nolna, you shall soon have me again."

The poor boy. Had he paid closer mind to the culture of the Land of Light and Dark, he would have known that to refuse a slice of yellow sunshine, a bowl of friendship, and a cup of laughter three consecutive times, without indicating to the friend that he should return before the new moon, is to flatly refuse the friendship forever and always; he would probably, at the very least, have invited N'Tho in for a minute or two. Too bad he did not. For that whole morning, door after door pushed at the heels of the young artist, until it became clear to him that he had somehow become anathema to the winged people. He walked home with stooped shoulders. "Well," he said to himself, "at least I've still got Nonah." But it soon occurred to him that he could not conjure an image of her face, and as he turned the knob of his door he finally admitted to himself that he couldn't remember her name. "But it must be in my journal," he thought, and dashed to his studio. He found his little self, with a round, full stomach and closed eyes, snoozing atop his much-reduced manuscript. "You little spawn of Hatsax! You Old-forsaken pup of a scuttlerat. You oily-lipped, foul, cretinous do—"

The little one shot up from his supine position and backed himself against the wall. "Yo, man, ice'n up yourself. You buggin, homeboy." But the young artist would have no more. He grabbed his letter opener and lunged at the little beast. Of course, he missed. "Look, man," the homunculus said, scrambling atop a lamp, "chill. All that salt you done layed down on them pages gonna kill me before you do. Your stuff's getting harder to eat every five minutes. I'ma be honest with you, man. Page sixty-three I simply could not get past my soup coolers."

The young artist hadn't realized he'd dropped the letter opener till he heard it clatter to the floor. "You've eaten sixty-two pages?"

"Sixty-five if you don't count page sixty-three. Th'ew that one away." The homunculus reached into his pocket, pulled out a tiny pipe, a tiny book of matches, lit the pipe, took a long deep puff, blew the smoke in the young artist's face, shook out the match, and squinted one black eye at his maker. "So, what you writing about, boy?" he said.

"You mean you don't even know?"

The little one slipped the matchbook back into his pocket, shuffled his feet a bit, and said, "Well, not really, but I am what I eat, I guess you could say."

The artist dropped into a chair and hung his head low. What was the use of fighting? he thought. He was clearly insane. His friends had abandoned him; it was probably too late to begin reading his work now, for if he could not remember his old love's name or the color of her hair or the shape of her smile, what was the use in fighting? This little version of himself, whether he be real or illusory, was, it seemed, all he had. The two of them sat till the sun began to cast its orange light in through the southern windows of his studio. The only sound that could be heard was the hiss and burble of the little one's pipe. Suddenly, the homunculus spoke. "Tell me something, Skippy," he said. "Whycome you never stopped to read what you wrote?"

The artist shrugged and sighed. "I don't know, exactly. Fear, perhaps? It's everything I've ever wanted to do, I've ever wanted to say. It's my whole life. It's about my lovely What's-Her-Name. It's . . . rather it could be — *could* have been, anyway, the greatest work ever created. Old One! There is something wonderful about it. And . . . and even if no one had ever liked it, why, even if no one had ever even read it, I know in my heart that it's changed me. It's done something to me. How all this has happened — how it resulted in you, I mean — I don't know, but I have just known it was a great work. So great, perhaps, that I knew that even I wouldn't be able to understand it." He let his head fall to the back of his chair, but kept his eyes on the little one. The little one sucked on his pipe, grimacing every now and then, but let several minutes go by before he said, "You hongry?"

"No."

"I'm hongry. You mind?"

The artist shrugged. The homunculus chuckled softly, took the pipe from his mouth, and knocked out the ashes on the artist's desk. "Yep," he said. "Look like to me this great work a yours is just about finito, buddy-bud. Ain' no sense in letting it go to waste. Sure you don't mind?"

The young man made no reply.

"So," said the homunculus, "you writing this here thing for the love of some woman, huh?" And then he turned to, gobbling, smacking, chewing with great heat. "Well," said the young artist, in a voice that could have been no more hollow had he spoken into a bucket while standing in the middle of a prayer chamber. "Well," said he, "at first I didn't think so. I never admitted it to myself, but the more I wrote the more it seemed so. But then the work itself became the thing. And I —" Out the corner of his eye he noted the flurry of movement as the little one fed himself. The leaves of the manuscript flew in a haze of motion, and the arms and hands of the homunculus appeared to multiply by twos and fours, so frenetically did he propel them. And by increments the little thing began to grow. At two hundred twenty-two pages he'd doubled in size, at four hundred forty-four he'd quadrupled. By now he was half the size of his maker. But the artist began to notice something more unsettling than this: The little man looked enormously uncomfortable; his arms seemed to move by themselves; every dozen pages or so he would feverishly glance up at his maker. His eyes seemed to say, stop me, why don't you! He looked nauseous with panic, but still he ate in a hail of movement. Finally, he was swallowing the eight hundred eighty-eighth page. He looked precisely, exactly, undeniably like his maker, inch for inch, whisker for whisker. The only differences between the two men were that one sat in a chair, the other on the desk, and one looked astonished and bemused, the other queasy and gray. The queasy one said, through trembling lips, "Y-you better read this motherfuh-fuh, man, 'cause —" Too late. He folded over as if cut in two, and vomited the entire manuscript, unchewed, unwrinkled, unripped, unsoggy, with the force of an unknotted water balloon. And he shrunk at a rate faster than he'd grown. And he disappeared in a puff of blue smoke. And he didn't come back.

The young artist began reading what he'd written almost immediately. Including page sixty-three. He never gave his double another thought. He read unceasingly for eight days and eight nights, one hundred eleven pages per day. When he finished, he floated the eight hundred eighty-eighth page onto the floor and sobbed till his temples pounded and his throat clamped nearly shut. He had taken no food and water for a week and a day, and, of course, fell gravely ill. He plunged into a well of sleep. A great fever swept through him, so great it was that it touched off a tremendous fire in his rooms, a fire which neither burned him nor even woke him. But all his work was lost.

On the ninth day he awoke and found his rooms whole, and cleaner than they had been in months. The doctor, whom his servants had called eight days before, felt his forehead, shook his hand, and wished him well. His chambermaid brought him a hearty meal of rice and sauce, fruit and vegetables. The next morning he made arrangements to return home. He packed all his possessions but searched in vain for his work. He moved the furniture this way and that way, but could find nothing.

He returned to the Realm and rented a small room near the Central Square. And he learned that during the one thousand seven hundred seventy-six days he had been gone, it had come to pass that his work was no longer regarded as the great thing it once had been. Other talented young artists had replaced him in the hearts of the people. But this did not perturb him. He had read his work, and he knew.

He spent the rest of his days working with Rafkhan the miller (whose daughter, they say, became a great impresario somewhere in the Outer Realm; Rafkhan never spoke her name from the day she left, so it never was remembered to the artist). He listened to the music of singers and composers, and studied, with admiration, the literature of the most popular writers and poets of the day. He visited museums. He bought inexpensive art, when he could, and decorated his room nicely. He married a young woman who had never heard of him. He raised seven sons and daughters. He took hardly any salt at all in his food.

He died at the age of one hundred sixteen, neither a happy man nor a sad man.

The Kind of Light
That Shines
on Texas

/ / / / / /

      I never liked Marvin Pruitt. Never liked him, never knew him, even though there were only three of us in the class. Three black kids. In our school there were fourteen classrooms of thirty-odd white kids (in '66, they considered Chicanos provisionally white) and three or four black kids. Primary school in primary colors. Neat division. Alphabetized. They didn't stick us in the back, or arrange us by degrees of hue, apart-heidlike. This was real integration, a ten-to-one ratio as tidy as upper-class landscaping. If it all worked, you could have ten white kids all to yourself. They could talk to you, get the feel of you, scrutinize you bone deep if they wanted to. They seldom wanted to, and that was fine with me for two reasons. The first was that their scrutiny was irritating. How do you comb your hair — why do you comb your hair — may I please touch your hair — were the kinds of questions they asked. This is no way to feel at home. The second reason was Marvin.

He embarrassed me. He smelled bad, was at least two grades behind, was hostile, dark skinned, homely, close-mouthed. I feared him for his size, pitied him for his dress, watched him all the time. Marveled at him, mystified, astonished, uneasy.

He had the habit of spitting on his right arm, juicing it down till it would glisten. He would start in immediately after taking his seat when we'd finished with the Pledge of Allegiance, "The Yellow Rose of Texas," "The Eyes of Texas Are upon You," and "Mistress Shady." Marvin would rub his spit-flecked arm with his left hand, rub and roll as if polishing an ebony pool cue. Then he would rest his head in the crook of his arm, sniffing, huffing deep like black-jacket boys huff bagsful of acrylics. After ten minutes or so, his eyes would close, heavy. He would sleep till recess. Mrs. Wickham would let him.

There was one other black kid in our class. A girl they called Ah-so. I never learned what she did to earn this name. There was nothing Asian about this big-shouldered girl. She was the tallest, heaviest kid in school. She was quiet, but I don't think any one of us was subtle or sophisticated enough to nickname our classmates according to any but physical attributes. Fat kids were called Porky or Butterball, skinny ones were called Stick or Ichabod. Ah-so was big, thick, and African. She would impassively sit, sullen, silent as Marvin. She wore the same dark blue pleated skirt every day, the same ruffled white blouse every day. Her skin always shone as if worked by Marvin's palms and fingers. I never spoke one word to her, nor she to me.

Of the three of us, Mrs. Wickham called only on Ah-so and me. Ah-so never answered one question, correctly or incorrectly, so far as I can recall. She wasn't stupid. When asked to read aloud she read well, seldom stumbling over long words, reading with humor and expression. But when Wickham asked her about Farmer Brown and how many cows, or the capital of Vermont, or the date of this war or that, Ah-so never spoke. Not one word. But you always felt she could have answered those questions if she'd wanted to. I sensed no tension, embarrassment, or anger in Ah-so's reticence. She simply refused to speak. There was something unshakable about her, some core so impenatrably solid, you got the feeling that if you stood too close to her she could eat your thoughts like a black star eats light. I didn't despise Ah-so as I despised Marvin. There was nothing malevolent about her. She sat like a great icon in the back of the classroom, tranquil, guarded, sealed up, watchful. She was close to sixteen, and it was my guess she'd given up on school. Perhaps she was just obliging the wishes of her family, sticking it out till the law could no longer reach her.

There were at least half a dozen older kids in our class. Besides Marvin and Ah-so there was Oakley, who sat behind me, whispering threats into my ear; Varna Willard with the large breasts; Eddie Limon, who played bass for a high school rock band; and Lawrence

Ridderbeck, who everyone said had a kid and a wife. You couldn't expect me to know anything about Texan educational practices of the 1960s, so I never knew why there were so many older kids in my sixth-grade class. After all, I was just a boy and had transferred into the school around midyear. My father, an air force sergeant, had been sent to Viet Nam. The air force sent my mother, my sister, Claire, and me to Connolly Air Force Base, which during the war housed "unaccompanied wives." I'd been to so many different schools in my short life that I ceased wondering about their differences. All I knew about the Texas schools is that they weren't afraid to flunk you.

Yet though I was only twelve then, I had a good idea why Wickham never once called on Marvin, why she let him snooze in the crook of his polished arm. I knew why she would press her lips together, and narrow her eyes at me whenever I correctly answered a question, rare as that was. I know why she badgered Ah-so with questions everyone knew Ah-so would never even consider answering. Wickham didn't like us. She wasn't gross about it, but it was clear she didn't want us around. She would prove her dislike day after day with little stories and jokes. "I just want to share with you all," she would say, "a little riddle my daughter told me at the supper table th'other day. Now, where do you go when you injure your knee?" Then one, two, or all three of her pets would say for the rest of us, "We don't know, Miz Wickham," in that skin-chilling way suck-asses speak, "where?" "Why, to Africa," Wickham would say, "where the knee grows."

The thirty-odd white kids would laugh, and I would look across the room at Marvin. He'd be asleep. I would glance back at Ah-so. She'd be sitting still as a projected image, staring down at her desk. I, myself, would smile at Wickham's stupid jokes, sometimes fake a laugh. I tried to show her that at least one of us was alive and alert, even though her jokes hurt. I sucked ass, too, I suppose. But I wanted her to understand more than anything that I was not like her other nigra children, that I was worthy of more than the non-attention and the negative attention she paid Marvin and Ah-so. I hated her, but never showed it. No one could safely contradict that woman. She knew all kinds of tricks to demean, control, and punish you. And she could swing her two-foot paddle as fluidly as a big-league slugger swings a bat. You didn't speak in Wickham's class unless she spoke to you first. You didn't chew gum, or wear "hood" hair. You didn't drag your feet, curse, pass notes, hold hands with the opposite sex. Most especially, you didn't say anything bad about the Aggies, Governor Connolly, LBJ, Sam Houston, or Waco. You did the forbidden and she would get you. It was that simple.

She never got me, though. Never gave her reason to. But she could have invented reasons. She did a lot of that. I can't be sure, but I used to think she pitied me because my father was in Viet Nam and my uncle A.J. had recently died there. Whenever she would tell one of her racist jokes, she would always glance at me, preface the joke with, "Now don't you nigra children take offense. This is all in fun, you know. I just want to share with you all something Coach Gilchrest told me th'other day." She would tell her joke, and glance at me again. I'd giggle, feeling a little queasy. "I'm half Irish," she would chuckle, "and you should hear some of those Irish jokes." She never told any, and I never really expected her to. I just did my Tom-thing. I kept my shoes shined, my desk neat, answered her questions as best I could, never brought gum to school, never cursed, never slept in class. I wanted to show her we were not all the same.

I tried to show them all, all thirty-odd, that I was different. It worked to some degree, but not very well. When some article was stolen from someone's locker or desk, Marvin, not I, was the first accused. I'd be second. Neither Marvin, nor Ah-so nor I were ever chosen for certain classroom honors — "Pledge leader," "flag holder," "noise monitor," "paper passer outer," but Mrs. Wickham once let me be "eraser duster." I was proud. I didn't even care about the cracks my fellow students made about my finally having turned the right color. I had done something that Marvin, in the deeps of his never-ending sleep, couldn't even dream of doing. Jack Preston, a kid who sat in front of me, asked me one day at recess whether I was embarrassed about Marvin. "Can you believe that guy?" I said. "He's like a pig or something. Makes me sick."

"Does it make you ashamed to be colored?"

"No," I said, but I meant yes. Yes, if you insist on thinking us all the same. Yes, if his faults are mine, his weaknesses inherent in me.

"I'd be," said Jack.

I made no reply. I was ashamed. Ashamed for not defending Marvin and ashamed that Marvin even existed. But if it had occurred to me, I would have asked Jack whether he was ashamed of being white because of Oakley. Oakley, "Oak Tree," Kelvin "Oak Tree" Oakley. He was sixteen and proud of it. He made it clear to everyone, including Wickham, that his life's ambition was to stay in school one more year, till he'd be old enough to enlist in the army. "Them slopes got my brother," he would say. "I'mna sign up and git me a few slopes. Gonna kill them bastards deader'n shit." Oakley, so far as anyone knew, was and always had been the oldest kid in his family. But no one contradicted him. He would, as anyone would tell you, "snap yer neck jest as soon as look at you." Not a boy in class, excepting Marvin and myself, had been able to avoid Oakley's pink bellies, Texas titty twisters, moon pie punches, or worse. He didn't bother Marvin, I suppose, because Marvin was closer to his size and age, and because Marvin spent five sixths of the school day asleep. Marvin probably never crossed Oakley's mind. And to say that Oakley hadn't bothered me is not to say he had no intention of ever doing so. In fact, this haphazard sketch of hairy fingers, slash of eyebrow, explosion of acne, elbows, and crooked teeth, swore almost daily that he'd like to kill me.

Naturally, I feared him. Though we were about the same height, he outweighed me by no less than forty pounds. He talked, stood, smoked, and swore like a man. No one, except for Mrs. Wickham, the principal, and the coach, ever laid a finger on him. And even Wickham knew that the hot lines she laid on him merely amused him. He would smile out at the class-room, goofy and bashful, as she laid down the two, five, or maximum ten strokes on him. Often he would wink, or surreptitiously flash us the thumb as Wickham worked on him. When she was finished, Oakley would walk so cool back to his seat you'd think he was on wheels. He'd slide into his chair, sniff the air, and say, "Somethin's burnin. Do y'all smell smoke? I swanee, I smell smoke and fahr back here." If he had made these cracks and never threatened me, I might have grown to admire Oakley, even liked him a little. But he hated me, and took every opportunity during the six-hour school day to make me aware of this. "Some Sambo's gittin his ass broke open one of these days," he'd mumble. "I wanna fight somebody. Need to keep in shape till I git to Nam."

I never said anything to him for the longest time. I pretended not to hear him, pretended not to notice his sour breath on my neck and ear. "Yep," he'd whisper. "Coonies keep y' in good shape for slope killin." Day in, day out, that's the kind of thing I'd pretend not to hear. But one day when the rain dropped down like lead balls, and the cold air made your skin look plucked, Oakley whispered to me, "My brother tells me it rains like this in Nam. Maybe I oughta go out at recess and break your ass open today. Nice and cool so you don't sweat. Nice and wet to clean up the blood." I said nothing for at least half a minute, then I turned half right and said, "Thought you said your brother was dead." Oakley, silent himself, for a time, poked me in the back with his pencil and hissed, "*Yer* dead." Wickham cut her eyes our way, and it was over.

It was hardest avoiding him in gym class. Especially when we played murderball. Oakley always aimed his throws at me. He threw with unblinking intensity, his teeth gritting, his neck veining, his face flushing, his black hair sweeping over one eye. He could throw hard, but the balls were squishy and harmless. In fact, I found his misses more intimidating than his hits. The balls would whizz by, thunder against the folded bleachers. They rattled as though a locomotive were passing through them. I would duck, dodge, leap as if he were throwing grenades. But he always hit me, sooner or later. And after a while I noticed that the other boys would avoid throwing at me, as if I belonged to Oakley.

One day, however, I was surprised to see that Oakley was throwing at everyone else but me. He was uncommonly accurate, too; kids were falling like tin cans. Since no one was throwing at me, I spent most of the game watching Oakley cut this one and that one down. Finally, he and I were the only ones left on the court. Try as he would, he couldn't hit me, nor I him.

Coach Gilchrest blew his whistle and told Oakley and me to bring the red rubber balls to the equipment locker. I was relieved I'd escaped Oakley's stinging throws for once. I was feeling triumphant, full of myself. As Oakley and I approached Gilchrest, I thought about saying something friendly to Oakley: Good game, Oak Tree, I would say. Before I could speak, though, Gilchrest said, "All right boys, there's five minutes left in the period. Y'all are so good, looks like, you're gonna have to play like men. No boundaries, no catch outs, and you gotta hit your opponent three times in order to win. Got me?"

We nodded.

"And you're gonna use these," said Gilchrest, pointing to three volleyballs at his feet. "And you better believe they're pumped full. Oates, you start at that end of the court. Oak Tree, you're at th'other end. Just like usual, I'll set the balls at mid-court, and when I blow my whistle I want y'all to haul your cheeks to the middle and th'ow for all you're worth. Got me?" Gilchrest nodded at our nods, then added, "Remember, no boundaries, right?"

I at my end, Oakley at his, Gilchrest blew his whistle. I was faster than Oakley and scooped up a ball before he'd covered three quarters of his side. I aimed, threw, and popped him right on the knee. "One–zip!" I heard Gilchrest shout. The ball bounced off his knee and shot right back into my hands. I hurried my throw and missed. Oakley bent down, clutched the two remaining balls. I remember being amazed that he could palm each ball, run full out, and throw left-handed or right-handed without a shade of awkwardness. I spun, ran, but one of Oakley's throws glanced off the back of my head. "One–one!" hollered Gilchrest. I fell and spun on my ass as the other ball came sailing at me. I caught it. "He's out!" I yelled. Gilchrest's voice boomed, "No catch outs. Three hits. Three hits." I leapt to my feet as Oakley scrambled across the floor for another ball. I chased him down, leapt, and heaved the ball hard as he drew himself erect. The ball hit him dead in the face, and he went down flat. He rolled around, cupping his hands over his nose. Gilchrest sped to his side, helped him to his feet, asked him whether he was OK. Blood flowed from Oakley's nose, dripped in startlingly bright spots on the floor, his shoes, Gilchrest's shirt. The coach removed Oakley's T-shirt and pressed it against the big kid's nose to stanch the bleeding. As they walked past me toward the office I mumbled an apology to Oakley, but couldn't catch his reply. "You watch your filthy mouth, boy," said Gilchrest to Oakley.

The locker room was unnaturally quiet as I stepped into its steamy atmosphere. Eyes clicked in my direction, looked away. After I was out of my shorts, had my towel wrapped around me, my shower kit in hand, Jack Preston and Brian Nailor approached me. Preston's hair was combed slick and plastic looking. Nailor's stood up like frozen flames. Nailor smiled at me with his big teeth and pale eyes. He poked my arm with a finger. "You fucked up," he said.

"I tried to apologize."

"Won't do you no good," said Preston.

"I swanee," said Nailor.

"It's part of the game," I said. "It was an accident. Wasn't my idea to use volleyballs."

"Don't matter," Preston said. "He's jest lookin for an excuse to fight you."

"I never done nothing to him."

"Don't matter," said Nailor. "He don't like you."

"Brian's right, Clint. He'd jest as soon kill you as look at you."

"I never done nothing to him."

"Look," said Preston, "I know him pretty good. And jest between you and me, it's 'cause you're a city boy —"

"Whadda you mean? I've never —"

"He don't like your clothes —"

"And he don't like the fancy way you talk in class."

"What fancy —"

"I'm tellin him, if you don't mind, Brian."

"Tell him then."

"He don't like the way you say 'tennis shoes' instead of sneakers. He don't like coloreds. A whole bunch a things, really."

"I never done nothing to him. He's got no reason —"

"*And*," said Nailor, grinning, "*and*, he says you're a stuck-up rich kid." Nailor's eyes had crow's-feet, bags beneath them. They were a man's eyes.

"My dad's a sergeant," I said.

"You chicken to fight him?" said Nailor.

"Yeah, Clint, don't be chicken. Jest go on and git it over with. He's whupped pert near ever'body else in the class. It ain't so bad."

"Might as well, Oates."

"Yeah, yer pretty skinny, but yer jest about his height. Jest git 'im in a headlock and don't let go."

"Goddamn," I said, "he's got no reason to —"

Their eyes shot right and I looked over my shoulder. Oakley stood at his locker, turning its tumblers. From where I stood I could see that a piece of cotton was wedged up one of his nostrils, and he already had the makings of a good shiner. His acne burned red like a fresh abrasion. He snapped the locker open and kicked his shoes off without sitting. Then he pulled off his shorts, revealing two paddle stripes on his ass. They were fresh red bars speckled with white, the white speckles being the reverse impression of the paddle's suction holes. He must not have watched his filthy mouth while in Gilchrest's presence. Behind me, I heard Preston and Nailor pad to their lockers.

Oakley spoke without turning around. "Somebody's gonna git his skinny black ass kicked, right today, right after school." He said it softly. He slipped his jock off, turned around. I looked away. Out the corner of my eye I saw him stride off, his hairy nakedness a weapon clearing the younger boys from his path. Just before he rounded the corner of the shower stalls, I threw my toilet kit to the floor and stammered, "I — I never did nothing to you, Oakley." He stopped, turned, stepped closer to me, wrapping his towel around himself. Sweat streamed down my rib cage. It felt like ice water. "You wanna go at it right now, boy?"

"I never did nothing to you." I felt tears in my eyes. I couldn't stop them even though I was blinking like mad. "Never."

He laughed. "You busted my nose, asshole."

"What about before? What'd I ever do to you?"

"See you after school, Coonie." Then he turned away, flashing his acne-spotted back like a semaphore. "Why?" I shouted. "Why you wanna fight me?" Oakley stopped and turned, folded his arms, leaned against a toilet stall. "Why you wanna fight *me*, Oakley?" I stepped over the bench. "What'd I do? Why me?" And then unconsciously, as if scratching, as if breathing, I walked toward Marvin, who stood a few feet from Oakley, combing his hair at the mirror. "Why not him?" I said. "How come you're after *me* and not *him?*" The room froze. Froze for a moment that was both evanescent and eternal, somewhere between an eye blink and a week in hell. No one moved, nothing happened; there was no sound at all. And then it was as if all of us at the same moment looked at Marvin. He just stood there, combing away, the only body in motion, I think. He combed his hair and combed it, as if seeing only his image, hearing only his comb scraping his scalp. I knew he'd heard me. There's no way he could not have heard me. But all he did was slide the comb into his pocket and walk out the door.

"I got no quarrel with Marvin," I heard Oakley say. I turned toward his voice, but he was already in the shower.

I was able to avoid Oakley at the end of the school day. I made my escape by asking Mrs. Wickham if I could go to the rest room.

" 'Rest room,' " Oakley mumbled. "It's a damn toilet, sissy."

"Clinton," said Mrs. Wickham. "Can you *not* wait till the bell rings? It's almost three o'clock."

"No ma'am," I said. "I won't make it."

"Well I should make you wait just to teach you to be more mindful about . . . hygiene . . . uh things." She sucked in her cheeks, squinted. "But I'm feeling charitable today. You may go." I immediately left the building, and got on the bus. "Ain't you a little early?" said the bus driver, swinging the door shut. "Just left the office," I said. The driver nodded, apparently not giving me a second thought. I had no idea why I'd told her I'd come from the office, or why she found it a satisfactory answer. Two minutes later the bus filled, rolled, and shook its way to Connolly Air Base. When I got home, my mother was sitting in the living room, smoking her Slims, watching her soap opera. She absently asked me how my day had gone and I told her fine. "Hear from Dad?" I said.

"No, but I'm sure he's fine." She always said that

when we hadn't heard from him in a while. I suppose she thought I was worried about him, or that I felt vulnerable without him. It was neither. I just wanted to discuss something with my mother that we both cared about. If I spoke with her about things that happened at school, or on my weekends, she'd listen with half an ear, say something like, "Is that so?" or "You don't say?" I couldn't stand that sort of thing. But when I mentioned my father, she treated me a bit more like an adult, or at least someone who was worth listening to. I didn't want to feel like a boy that afternoon. As I turned from my mother and walked down the hall I thought about the day my father left for Viet Nam. Sharp in his uniform, sure behind his aviator specs, he slipped a cigar from his pocket and stuck it in mine. "Not till I get back," he said. "We'll have us one when we go fishing. Just you and me, out on the lake all day, smoking and casting and sitting. Don't let Mama see it. Put it in y'back pocket." He hugged me, shook my hand, and told me I was the man of the house now. He told me he was depending on me to take good care of my mother and sister. "Don't you let me down, now, hear?" And he tapped his thick finger on my chest. "You almost as big as me. Boy, you something else." I believed him when he told me those things. My heart swelled big enough to swallow my father, my mother, Claire. I loved, feared, and respected myself, my manhood. That day I could have put all of Waco, Texas, in my heart. And it wasn't till about three months later that I discovered I really wasn't the man of the house, that my mother and sister, as they always had, were taking care of me.

For a brief moment I considered telling my mother about what had happened at school that day, but for one thing, she was deep down in the halls of *General Hospital*, and never paid you much mind till it was over. For another thing, I just wasn't the kind of person — I'm still not, really — to discuss my problems with anyone. Like my father I kept things to myself, talked about my problems only in retrospect. Since my father wasn't around I consciously wanted to be like him, doubly like him, I could say. I wanted to be the man of the house in some respect, even if it had to be in an inward way. I went to my room, changed my clothes, and laid out my homework. I couldn't focus on it. I thought about Marvin, what I'd said about him or done to him — I couldn't tell which. I'd done something to him, said something about him; said something about and done something to myself. *How come you're after* me *and not* him? I kept trying to tell myself I hadn't meant it that way. *That* way. I thought about approaching Marvin, telling him what I really meant was that he was more Oakley's age and weight than I. I would tell him I meant I was no match for Oakley. *See, Marvin, what I meant was that he wants to fight a colored guy, but is afraid to fight you 'cause you could beat him.* But try as I did, I couldn't for a moment convince myself that Marvin would believe me. I meant it *that* way and no other. Everybody heard. Everybody knew. That afternoon I forced myself to confront the notion that tomorrow I would probably have to fight both Oakley and Marvin. I'd have to be two men.

I rose from my desk and walked to the window. The light made my skin look orange, and I started thinking about what Wickham had told us once about light. She said that oranges and apples, leaves and flowers, the whole multicolored world, was not what it appeared to be. The colors we see, she said, look like they do only because of the light or ray that shines on them. "The color of the thing isn't what you see, but the light that's reflected off it." Then she shut out the lights and shone a white light lamp on a prism. We watched the pale splay of colors on the projector screen; some people oohed and aahed. Suddenly, she switched on a black light and the color of everything changed. The prism colors vanished, Wickham's arms were purple, the buttons of her dress were as orange as hot coals, rather than the blue they had been only seconds before. We were all very quiet. "Nothing," she said, after a while, "is really what it appears to be." I didn't really understand then. But as I stood at the window, gazing at my orange skin, I wondered what kind of light I could shine on Marvin, Oakley, and me that would reveal us as the same.

I sat down and stared at my arms. They were dark brown again. I worked up a bit of saliva under my tongue and spat on my left arm. I spat again, then rubbed the spittle into it, polishing, working till my arm grew warm. As I spat, and rubbed, I wondered why Marvin did this weird, nasty thing to himself, day after day. Was he trying to rub away the black, or deepen it, doll it up? And if he did this weird nasty thing for a hundred years, would he spit-shine himself invisible, rolling away the eggplant skin, revealing the scarlet muscle, blue vein, pink and yellow tendon, white bone? Then disappear? Seen through, all colors, no colors. Spitting and rubbing. Is this the way you do it? I leaned forward, sniffed the arm. It smelled vaguely of mayonnaise. After an hour or so, I fell asleep.

I saw Oakley the second I stepped off the bus the next morning. He stood outside the gym in his usual black penny loafers, white socks, high-water jeans, T-shirt, and black jacket. Nailor stood with him, his big teeth spread across his bottom lip like playing cards. If there was anyone I felt like fighting, that day, it was Nailor. But I wanted to put off fighting for as long as I could. I stepped toward the gymnasium, thinking that I shouldn't run, but if I hurried I could beat Oakley to the door and secure myself near Gilchrest's office. But the moment I stepped into the gym, I felt Oakley's broad palm clap down on my shoulder. "Might as well stay out here, Coonie," he said. "I need me a little target practice." I turned to face him and he slapped me, one-two, with the back, then the palm of his hand, as I'd seen Bogart do to Peter Lorre in *The Maltese Falcon*. My heart went wild. I could scarcely breathe. I couldn't swallow.

"Call me a nigger," I said. I have no idea what made me say this. All I know is that it kept me from crying. "Call me a nigger, Oakley."

"Fuck you, ya black-ass slope." He slapped me again, scratching my eye. "I don't do what coonies tell me."

"Call me a nigger."

"Outside, Coonie."

"Call me one. Go ahead!"

He lifted his hand to slap me again, but before his arm could swing my way, Marvin Pruitt came from behind me and calmly pushed me aside. "Git out my way, boy," he said. And he slugged Oakley on the side of his head. Oakley stumbled back, stiff-legged. His eyes were big. Marvin hit him twice more, once again to the side of the head, once to the nose. Oakley went down and stayed down. Though blood was drawn, whistles blowing, fingers pointing, kids hollering, Marvin just stood there, staring at me with cool eyes. He spat on the ground, licked his lips, and just stared at me, till Coach Gilchrest and Mr. Calderon tackled him and violently carried him away. He never struggled, never took his eyes off me.

Nailor and Mrs. Wickham helped Oakley to his feet. His already fattened nose bled and swelled so that I had to look away. He looked around, bemused, wall-eyed, maybe scared. It was apparent he had no idea how bad he was hurt. He didn't blink. He didn't even touch his nose. He didn't look like he knew much of anything. He looked at me, looked me dead in the eye, in fact, but didn't seem to recognize me.

That morning, like all other mornings, we said the Pledge of Allegiance, sang "The Yellow Rose of Texas," "The Eyes of Texas Are upon You," and "Mistress Shady." The room stood strangely empty without Oakley, and without Marvin, but at the same time you could feel their presence more intensely somehow. I felt like I did when I'd walk into my mother's room and could smell my father's cigars or cologne. He was more palpable, in certain respects, than when there in actual flesh. For some reason, I turned to look at Ah-so, and just this once I let my eyes linger on her face. She had a very gentle-looking face, really. That surprised me. She must have felt my eyes on her because she glanced up at me for a second and smiled, white teeth, downcast eyes. Such a pretty smile. That surprised me too. She held it for a few seconds, then let it fade. She looked down at her desk, and sat still as a photograph.

Roscoe in Hell

/ / / / / /

Melvin look at his wristwatch, tap his foot on the floor like we been waiting forever. "Jesus Christ, man," he say, "we been standing here f' damn near fi'teen minutes. What is this? Everywhere you go down here it's hurry up and wait. Right?" Then he wink at me.

"I guess," I say back. "Maybe we ought to knock again." I knock on the door as hard as I can and stand back and we wait. Then this real deep voice on the other side say, "Coooome in, y'all," like that gorilla-voice brother who sing bass for the Persuasions. I open the door real slow and Mel and me steps inside. The place is dark. Real quiet. It kinda give me the williams, if you know what I mean. Melvin nudge me on my arm. "Hello?" I say. But I get no answer. We wait for maybe about five minutes, and so I say, "Maybe we ought to check out them other places you was talking about first, then maybe come back over here later." Melvin don't say nothing, he just light up a cigar and act like he prepared to wait all day, if need be.

All of a sudden, though, a light pops on, and all these well-dressed-up people jumps outta nowhere, and they all screaming at us.

"Surprise!"

It's a party. There's blue and black and red and green streamers unrolling all over the damn place, and people blowing horns and whistles and making all kinds of noise. Most of 'em still running around doing last-minute decorating, wiping down tables, laying out food. Every so often folks wave and wink, nod at me and whatnot, but when any of 'em tries to stop and talk to me, Melvin shake his head, point somewheres, and say, "Plenty a time for that, y'all. Get it right for the man. Make it right. Make it right." Then he clap his rubber-looking hands together and say, "Hurr' up, now, hurr' up. Y'all shoulda had this done at eight o'clock. Y'all act like y'ain't got no sense of time." And folks is cracking up behind that one. I am too. Even though I ain't been here all that long, I know that time don't mean a thing to nobody.

The joint's packed with all kind of people. Normal people, not like Melvin. Don't get me wrong, now. Melvin cool. He's really helped me out down here, and he very hip, too. Stone def. But he ugly. The man so black he could cast a shadow in a coal mine. I ain't got nothing against dark skin. Matter a fact I'm pretty chocolate my own self, but Melvin, well one look at him

and you think he made out of tire rubber. And when I
say ugly, I mean he put the U in ugly. He all baggy and
scrunched down like he boneless. Look like stacks and
stacks of pancakes. Told me he used to be tall, six foot
eight, or something like that. Brother was a power
forward for some ABA team back in the seventies.
"Woulda made the NB, too, if I hadn'ta died," he told
me. "But I'm glad I didn't live, to tell you the truth. I'm
glad I didn't continue to be no slave to the entertain-
ment junkieism of the masses, letting them exploit my
black ass for their wanton pleasures. Sheeit, fuck their
wanton asses."

"So what happened?" I ast him. "You got killed in a
trash compactor, or something?"

"Naw-ah, man. Heart attack."

"Then whycome you all scrunched down like that?"
Melvin heave on his Corona.

"Well," he say, "first thing I asked for when I got
here was to be four eight instead of six eight. You in hell
now, brother. You can be whatever you wanna be here.
For me, being six eight, black, with skillet-size hands
and a forty-eight-inch vertical leap was a curse. For
you, I don't know. Whatever you want, it's cool. You
free now, brother. Free." Didn't know what to think of
that, but I did ast him why I'm here in the first place.
All he said back was, "Nothing to it. Everybody go to
hell, Roscoe."

Anyway, like I'm saying, this room's full of all these
real nice-looking people, and I figure I'm gonna have a

pretty chill time here. And the room's like a office. There's desks, typewriters, copying machines, fifty-button telephones, word processors, fax machines, and all that, but they all pushed up against the walls, out the way. In the middle of the room they got these three big tables crammed with all this liquor and grub. They got Gilbey's, Wolfschmidt, Ron Rico, Dewar's, Crown Royal, Jim Beam, Kahlua, Johnnie Red, and Johnnie Black. There's imported beer frosting down in big silver tubs, little sissy sandwiches made with black bread, brown bread, white bread. They got this red, rolled up fishy-smelling shit called lox. They got about four kind of olives, barbecued hot wings, meatballs wrapped in bacon, sweet pickles, and this funky-smelling French cheese that look like some kind of pie. Melvin stand next to me with his arms folded over his chest, and he just grinning proud, like he done cooked it all hisself. "That right there?" he say, pointing to some funny-looking brown shrooms. "That's what you call *chantrelles*. Twelve ninety-five a pound, brother."

"What?"

"That's right. But that ain't nothing. You see them shrooms there, the ones look like dicks? They called morels, one twenty-five a pound."

"Dollars?"

"Mmm-hmm."

"A pound?"

"Mmm-hmm." And then he raise up on his toes, like he in church, and fend to get happy. He look around at the people still getting the place ready. Ugly as he is, he one cool Samuel.

"They get you high?" I say.

"Naw, but don't you worry, 'Scoe. There be lotsa feel-good down here."

After they done readying the place, folks comes up to me and shakes my hand, hug me like we old buddies. Some big fat, red-face dude in a powder blue leisure suit slides up to me, slap me on the back, and shove a drink in my hand. "Good ta see ya. Nice ta meet ya," he say. "Nice ta have ya. Nice ta greet ya," and he start cracking up behind that weak rap, like he some kind of comedy genius. His breath stink something fierce, but I don't care. I knock the drink down and it burn all the way to my gut. "Rrraahh," I say. "Gimme some more, homeboy." And he do. I never did drink much before. Mama killed herself drinking, and I promised my Aunt Shawnette I wouldn't do the same thing to myself. I stayed away from just about everything but beer. But if it wasn't for herbs and rock, I don't have no idea what I woulda did. A man can't live without getting high. I gotta admit I shouldn't'a got into the bidness, but drugging ain't cheap. You be a fool if you got the habit and don't sell. And why not? Getting blazed is natural. That's one thing I could never get Aunt Shawnette to understand, with her tired red wig and little silly-ass Bible with the zipper. Folks got to get high sometimes. It's natural. "Natural," she'd say, "Roscoe, boy, death's natural too. You wanna be natural like your mother, just go right on ahead."

"Just 'cause you don't get high —"

"And don't you forget your father used to get natural till he got with the Lord. And my life's got nothing to do with nothing. Don't look at my life as an example, look at your mother's, may she rest in peace."

"Pops quit getting high 'cause —"

Then she'd wag that zippered Bible in my mug and say, "Because of this, and nothing else. Nothing else. Now promise me on this book that you'll stay away from that natural disaster that killed your mother. Come on now, Roscoe. On the book."

So I did it. Didn't mean nothing. Even though it hurt me just as much as it did Shawnette to see Moms get juiced down damn near every night, I didn't see things that way. Shawnette never understood, but I did. I didn't enjoy seeing my mama stumble into the house half blind, half funny, half scary, half ugly. Don't nobody wanna see they mom fall on the living-room floor, throw up, and sleep in her own mess. Don't nobody wanna read in the paper about how they mama got so sliced one night that she couldn't feel a forty-degree-below chill-factor wind cut into her so bad she lost three fingers and a foot. And don't nobody like to talk about they mama dying. Period. But at the same time don't nobody want no father who so proud sober that he step over his own drunk wife when she laying on the living-room rug in her own mess. Step over her and

go right to bed, saying, "And I defy any one of y'all to
help her up. Let her sleep in her own mess. Maybe
she'll wake up and be so disgusted with herself, she'll
stop shaming the family." And don't nobody want no
Aunt Shawnette wagging no zippered Bible in nobody's
face. I didn't like none of that shit, but I did understand
my mama. At least I did understand.

"Rrraahh," I go when the second drink flame on down.
Right then, somebody turn on the stereo and the tune
"What You See Is What You Get" come on. Melvin cut
a bad move across the floor and wrap his arm around
my waist and sing, "Some people . . . are made of
plastic."

And I hook my arm around his shoulder, singing,
"And you know some people . . . are made a wood."

"Some people," say the fat man, slapping his big old
meat hook on my shoulder, "have hearts a stone."

And I say, "Some people . . . are up to no good."
And we just about die laughing. I stand there, sipping
my drink, bouncing to the music, tapping my foot.
Some of that old-timey shit ain't too bad. I wouldn't
mind if they threw down some L.L. or some DMC or
NWA, but this old stuff all right. Real nice speakers,
too. If I wasn't in hell they be mine. I'd take the whole
set before these dickheads could blink. Melvin tap me
on the shoulder and point up to this great big sign on
the wall across the room, and it say WELCOME TO
HELL, MR. CRANDEL. Melvin nudge me again and

nod his head to the side for me to bend down so he can say something to me. "This is better'n the Lake of Fire, huh, 'Scoe?"

"You ain't buggin', homegrown. Got the Sea a Boiling Blood beat by a mile, too. Cain't understand why them people even be in that motherfucka."

"Yes sir, and you can stay here, if you want. But like I told you at the front desk, you sign on here and you got to stay. And as the new man your job would be to keep these folks happy. Course, if you can't handle the job —"

"Don't sound so hard to me."

"True, but you told me you wasn't much of a partyboy when you was back in the world."

"I guess not. Not really. Hey, Melvin?"

"Mmm?"

"How many other places is there down here?"

"That's just what I was gonna tell you. You got the Sea of Boiling Blood, the Lake of Fire, the Shit Storm Room, Smegma City, the Acid Pools, the Endless Gauntlet, the Disection/Resection Clinic — that's where I started before I got promoted to Assistant Concierge. But anyway, you got Cannibal Gardens, the —"

"Wait a second. Wait a second. Wait a second. Them places sound fucked up. Why would anybody choose them places over this one? Seem like to me this place oughta have a couple billion folks in it."

"Well, that ain't simple to answer, little bro'. See,

them other places ain't so bad. Now you take the Sea, for example. The shit's hard to look at, but the beach is nice, and them daily baths, they tell me, make your sex life hotter than a pepper-sauce enema. And you ain't never tasted chitlins till you been to Cannibal Gardens."

"Eeew."

"Strokes for folks."

"Yeah, well it just don't make no sense to me."

Melvin take a cigar from his coat pocket, fire it up, and pull on it hard, two, three times. "Don't know for sure, little brother," he say, "but most of the people in the Sea of Boiling Blood and the Lake of Fire's preachers, evangelists, deacons, rabbis, priests, and so forth. I guess after oppressing the masses with the opium of religion, they need to repent for the materiality of their heretofore bullshit. Religion is the sty of the oppressed, brother. It's for folks who ain't found themselves or lost themselves — that's Marx talking, not me — but anyway, I guess the Sea and the Lake is for folks who can't break that wanton cycle." Then he puff two, three more times. "Like I say, they some wanton motherfuckas."

"Yeah," I say, "I guess you right. Word."

Mel a hopping dude, and he damn smart. I like him. He took real good care a me when I first got here. Funny how I got here. I don't remember how much rock I smoked or anything like that, and I'm not sure who it was took me to Denver General. Shawnette, I think it was. I do remember some of the emergency-room things, and then I was floating. And dig, it was nice 'cause that's what you get high for. Floating. There. You know? I was warm, and relaxed, and all I'm thinking about is seeing Moms. There, like I never was before. Then I do see Moms. She looked so young, I almost didn't recognize her at first. "I'm There, Mama," I said, and she said, "You There, baby." Then next thing I know, I'm falling through eight plates of glass. The glass didn't break, though. Just sorta fell through it like they was soap bubbles. I fell on through and landed on my feet. I was standing right at the front desk. I rang the bell, like it was the most natural thing on earth, and there was Melvin, with his radial-colored self. Didn't even ask the man where I was; I just knew. Melvin handed me a pen and I signed the register. First thing he did was take my measurements and get me a three-piece. Everybody in hell wear three-pieces, Melvin told me.

I looks good in it, and everybody tell me I'm the cleanest brother in the joint. I look around myself, at all the wild going-ons around the room. The place packed with beautiful women, wiggling and jiggling and running around in dresses that look like they tattooed on, and some of 'em dancing in fronta me, saying, "Come on, come on, come on" with they hands and asses and rolling, rolling, rolling hips, and there's all this food, which costed somebody some wide green, and all these lights that dance to the music, and herb burning, and sweet rock cooking, and somebody throws down some Kool Moe Dee, saying, "Wild Wild West! Wild Wild Wild West!" and my heart tumbling in my chest just like it was when I O.D.'d. And I remember. My heart bouncing like a basketball, that doctor pounding on my chest at Denver General, saying, "Come on, come on, come on. Don't you dare! Don't you dare! You're too young. Come on, come on, come on," but I wasn't listening. Sure, I heard the man, but I wasn't listening, 'cause I knew what Moms knew. I knew there wasn't no high like too high, and I saw just how high too high was and I wasn't scared. Then my heart was just purring like a cat, and my chest felt solid as a wood tea chest. I felt me slip out myself and, man, I felt fresh. Fresh. Word. I felt fresh. I kept on climbing higher, and up, and up, until I couldn't tell up from down. I was just hanging, like steam, like temperature. "There," I said. "There."

And just like at the hospital, where they was saying come on, come on, it got me to thinking, the way these babes is calling me in with all them swerves, curves, and fingernails flashing — and my being dead with nothing to lose and so forth — that I wasn't There yet. That There in the world ain't nothing compared to There in hell. *Come on, come on, come on!* That's what the women say to me and the smoke say to me, the lights, the jams, the grub say to me — the women, the smoke, the lights, the jams, the grub, saying come on, come on, come on, come on, come on, so I slam down one more drink and "Rrraahh! Sign me up, Mel, this my kind of hell." He hand me a joint, flame it on for me, nod, and say, "Plenty of time for that, brother, take your sweet-ass time." I pull on the joint, moonwalk up to this light-skin freckle-face babe who revolving it in my face, and do Da Butt. The herb in my lungs and in my brain, and it's good, too. The freckle-face babe look good, but I can tell she all dance and no talk. Not usually the kind of broad I take much interest in. They don't understand me and I don't understand them. I like someone who read and like to talk about books, and I notice most women bored by dudes like me. I can't help it, though. That's how Moms brought me up. She wasn't like that with my brother, Whodini, whose real name Lonnie, or my sister, Tanya — whose real name Princess Pain-in-the-Ass — just me. I guess you could say I was special.

I was real sick as a kid, skinny, built like tweezers and pipe cleaners. Used to get nosebleeds a lot, and two, three times I threw up blood. Scared Moms something serious, but I don't really know what was wrong with me. Moms never took me to no doctors; she didn't trust 'em. She'd just keep me home from school and hold my hand while I laid in bed. She'd bring me Tang and ginger ale and noodle soup. And she'd always read to me. Always. She read me all kinds of stuff — Dickens, Harvey comic books, Jean Toomer, magazines with titles like *True Love* and *True Romance*, cookbooks, newspapers. Everything, really. I don't know how or why, but I'd always get better. She'd just read, read, read, till I'd get better. Mom could always tell, too, before I'd even say a word. She'd just stop reading, feel my head, and say, "There, young man. You There." And she'd pat my arm, stagger away, drunk as she could be, close my door, and I'd go to sleep. It always worked.

After I turned ten or so, my health got better. But I'd play sick every once in a while so she'd read for me. Like when it was cold in the morning, and the snow be piling up outside in flakes as big as quarters, I'd climb out of bed, look out the window, and just say, "Sheeit." Go back into bed. Mama'd come into my room to ask me why wasn't I up. "Sick," I'd say, and she always knew I wasn't. At first I'd think she was mad. She was almost always hung over, and her eyes'd be all red and swole up, her Afro'd be flat in the back, her robe be buttoned up all wrong. She'd still have some makeup on around her eyes, but it'd be all smeared around. Made her look a whole lot meaner than she was. "You ain't sick, boy," she'd say, feeling my head.

"I might not be sick, Mama, but I don't feel so good."

"What's wrong?" she'd say.

"Wanna find out what happened with Jackie and Steve."

"Who?"

"Them two people you read me about last week. The ones whose unspoke pain so deep that every night was a vacuum of silence and every day a desert of stillness."

"In *Romance?*"

"That's the one."

"Lord, boy, I . . ." She'd shove her hands into her pockets and sigh, look down at her feet. "How you doing in school?" she'd say.

"Same. Good."

"You being for real, boy?"

"Yes."

"And if you come home with a 'D' or worse on your report card?"

"Me?"

"Yes, you."

"If that happen, you don't have to read to me if I ever get sick for real."

Then, walking out the room, she'd say she didn't know what she was gonna do with me. But I knew. She was gonna bring me some Tang — and maybe a sweet roll 'cause I wasn't really sick — and she was gonna bring a little nip and a pack of Kools for herself. She was gonna read me about Jackie and Steve, and maybe, after that, Heathcliff and Catherine or Archie and Veronica. And I'd listen to her voice get rough with cigarettes and smooth with liquor, deep for the man parts and sweet for the woman parts. She was gonna hold my hand, squeeze it when the man got cruel, loosen when the woman got cold, let go when the love faded, drag on the Kool, taste the liquor, and turn the page. With every

nip she took in, Jackie and Steve, Heathcliff and Catherine, Archie and Veronica would get realer and realer,
flesh out and fill up. My room would fade away, and
we'd be somewhere else, see all these new faces, know
all these new secrets. I'd know them better than I knew
my brother or sister or friends, or even myself. Moms
would get drunker, they would get realer, and then her
voice'd start to croak, then crumble, then shut down.
She'd close up the book and just sit there for a long
time. Staring. Not saying a word. She was somewhere
else. I would roll to my side, start drifting off to sleep,
wondering how Moms did it, how she could be all them
people, understand their pain, speak in all them voices,
make her own self disappear. "You There," she'd say,
stand up, and close the door.

Well anyway, this place is really popping, right? And
when I finish dancing, everybody crowd around me
and shake my hand, high-five me, back-five me, back
pat me. This blade-face whiteboy ease up to me and
say, "Bitchin, dude. Where'd you learn to move like
that? Jee-zuz, could you show me that step?" "Ain't
nothing," I say back. "Just keep your eye my way next
time I'm on the floor." Then this Chinese-looking babe
in baggy pants and a tube top come my way and ask me
where I got the bad three-piece I'm wearing, and I tell
her, "Front desk, same as everybody else. Standard
issue, you know?" But she say, "Yeah, but hardly anyone wears them. If they all looked as good in theirs as

you do in yours I'd break my neck again just looking at them. But I'm keeping my eyes on you, hon." And she wink at me. Next thing that happen is this sweet-looking redhead babe in a pink miniskirt and pink high heels fight her way up to me through the crowd, leap up, throw her arms around my neck, lays on me the biggest, wettest kiss I ever had. She fine, and you ain't got to be a Einstein to know what she want. "Oh, Mr. Crandel," she say, "you're the person we've been wait-ing for, for so long. Something tells me you're gonna make us so happy. Thank you for dying so young, Mr. Crandel. We all think it was so brave of you to die so young for us."

"Huh, well, I wouldn't call O.D.'ing volunteering, exactly."

Everbody laugh they ass off when I say this. It surprises me.

"Well," she say, and wrap her leg around me, "what-ever you wanna call it, baby. We weren't expecting you for another seven years." Then she grind her thing up on my leg and my johnson say, "Hello! What's this?" But in the back a my mind, I'm kinda upset by what she said. *Another seven years?* I say to myself. *That mean I woulda only lived to be twenty-seven. Twenty-seven? Damn. I mean I was in shape, too. Played a lot of ball. Didn't smoke cigarettes. Never got into no gunplay. Used rubbers most of the time. Damn.* And it kinda mystify me that she make it sound like this whole throwdown been waiting for me. Melvin told me I was free, and I could choose wherever I wanna be in this place. I look around for Melvin to ask him about all this, but he ain't nowhere to be seen. But I ain't signed no papers yet, so I know he ain't gone yet.

I can't keep my mind behind this stuff about dying, since, for one thing, it don't make no difference no way, and for another, this babe got her leg all wrapped around me and she winding and grinding like she fend to throw sparks. "Where the bedroom at?" I say, and next thing you know, she leading me across the room. We slip into a broom closet, where they got this cot. This fat red candle's the only light in the room, and cherry incense smoke is twisting in the air. Ol' Red pull me down on top of her and I turned that stuff out. Like my brother, Whodini, say, I restructured the woman's anatomy. I mean, two minutes after I was buckling up my belt she was rattling, just laying there twitching. When I step out the place, there's a line of women outside, and the first one, a bald-headed sister who got on a shiny silver jacket and big globe earrings, push me back into the room. She weird looking, but make my girlfriend Danita look like a box of sticks. Naw, that ain't right. Danita was maybe too skinny and had bad skin, but she was OK for a while. But me and the bald-head babe do things I bet even pimps dream about, things I never knew could be done, things I don't think Danita woulda dug. And then I do it a few more times, with a few more babes, till Mr. Johnson feel like he weigh about four, five pounds. I can't hold up no more so tell 'em I need some kinda break and step out into the wild light of the main room.

Melvin right. I never got into parties back in the world. It wasn't that I didn't like good food, and music and all that. I just never liked people all that much. Maybe they didn't like me, I guess. I was pretty dull when you got down to it, kept my nose in books, never had a whole lot to say to folks. Lot of the people I knew thought I belonged to a gang. I didn't. I ran with some of them so-called Crips, 'cause my brother, Whodini, had serious rank in the chapter in Denver, and most of them boys knew where to find first-class rock. It was Whodini got me started on herb and rock. It was a little bit after he got out of jail the first time. Him and a couple dudes went upside some old white man's head with golf clubs and took fourteen bucks off him. I myself couldn't believe it. I mean golf clubs. Golf clubs. For fourteen gotdamn dollars and zero cent. Anyway, Who only did two and a half years behind that nonsense, and got out when I was a sophomore in high school. Surprised everybody to see him, but that was Who. Never said nothing to no one. Just showed up one day on the front stoop, acting as casual and loose as a Armani jacket. I was the only one home at the time 'cause Pops was working O.T. — as usual — Moms was out drinking somewhere, and Tanya — I don't know where she was, with her little knock-kneed self. "Hey, young blood," said Whodini from behind these shades so dark you'd think they was shoe heels.

"Damn! Lonnie! You escape, man?"

I wanted to hug him, but he couldn'ta played that. Instead I gave him a serious quadruple high five.

"Escape? Sheeuh, boy, why would I wanna escape from the only home I got?"

I didn't know how to answer that, 'cause it was true. Pops told Whodini that if he saw the boy around the house he'd tear him a new asshole. Pops didn't just say things so you could hear his soup coolers flap. He'da shot Whodini without blinking. "Pops ain't home," I said. "You can come in if you want."

"Mama home?"

"No."

"No need to come in, then. Let's go."

I ast him, go where, and he said over to his friend Fat Crawford's place. Then I told him I couldn't 'cause I had books to hit, but he said fuck that, and I said that was easy for a ninth-grade dropout to say, and he got all heartstring on me, saying he been in the joint for two and a half years, and how I'm his little brother and if anybody ought to be glad to see him it should be me, so I said, "How long you staying over there?"

"I'm bagging there, but I'll bring you back by six." And then we stepped into the deffest '84 New Yorker I ever seen, and we rolled on over to Fat Crawford's.

P-bud, Sgt. Rex, and Khalifa was all there. All these boys was Crips. I wasn't really close to none of 'em, though. Ganging don't mean nothing. It's bullshit. You hang out when they tell you to, do what they tell you to. I don't play that. I mean it ain't exactly dangerous to cut loose when you in a town like Denver. Like, if I was in L.A. or New York or something, well, it's different. Besides, I don't do what nobody — nobody — say. That's why I quit school. That's why I even left home after a while. They used to call me the Lone Roscoe. I went to parties, but I usually just sat there and drank a malt liquor or three. Never said shit to no one. Whenever somebody'd pass by where I was sitting, I'd nod, they'd nod, and that'd be that. That's pretty much how the afternoon went at Fat Crawford's, except it wasn't just liquor there. Crawford broke out some herb, Whodini broke out the rock. If I said I wasn't scared, I'd be lying. I felt sick, as a matter of fact. My hands was cold, and I was trembling. I felt sicker and sicker as the pipe kept getting closer. I tried to tell Whodini with my eyes that I didn't want none of that crap, but he was too high to pay me no mind, and with them shoe heels over his eyes I didn't figure he could see me anyway. Finally the pipe got to me. P-bud dropped a rock in and held the Cricket over the bowl for me. I played it chill and huffed. I liked it. I liked it. I felt morning pink and down-jacket warm. I felt like God, Conan, and the Invisible Man. I felt like every good book Moms ever read me. I felt cartoon, speed, lightning, polished glass, love, altitude, bullet, tears, clouds, flames, peaches, angels, water. Word. I liked it.

"Peep, homeboy," said Fat Crawford while I was sailing. "You like this stuff?" I told him I did. He sat back and grinned, his gheri curls all greasy, like he done soaked his head in a pot of my mama's pig knuckles. Big Negro sat back, grinning with a grin as big a bumper on a '84 New Yorker. "Everybody do," he said. "Everybody do." And then he leaned forward, threading his thick fingers together. "You know how your brother got that ride out there? After two days out the slam?" And before I could tell him no I didn't, he said, "You know how he got that four-hundred-dollar suit, that Rolex, that def ring he got on, them bad shoes?"

"He sell crack," I said.

Fat Crawford fell back laughing, spread his arms out on the couch. "Man, you one ready little dude," he said. "You on it, boy. You on it. Awright, now see can you answer me this —"

"You want me to sell the shit too."

Which made Fat Crawford crack up more. He leaned forward. "Hey, Who," he said. "When you said this boy was on it you wasn't lying, hometown. He on it."

"Just like me," said Whodini.

Crawford turned his fat head my way. "So what you gon' do, little man? You wanna be Crip?"

"No," I said.

"So you don't need the money, huh?"

"Sure I do. I'll sell, but I won't join y'all's gang."

"Naw, naw, naw, see. You wanna peddle the shit you got to do it from the inside."

Fat Crawford didn't know who he was talking to. I went home that night with two ounces of rock, a quarter pound of herb, and a pipe. First thing I did was flame up some herb, then some rock, grab a copy of *Captain Blackman* by John A. Williams, and read that motherfucka in two.

All over the room you hear corks popping, glasses being filled, loud laughing from the men, high-pitched screeching from the women. The party's in high gear, and when them pipes come my way, I'm flying. Melvin slide up to me with his rubber self and tap me on the shoulder. "Hey, 'Scoe," he say, "don't you think you oughta make a speech or something, brother?"

"Speech? What kinda speech? What for?"

"Just say whatever come into your mind, man. These good folks. The lumpen masses. They don't see a man like you every day. They love you."

"Lumpy, huh? Think I should?"

"Sure. Sure."

"Whatever come to my mind?"

"Preach, now. Preach."

"Why I'm so special? I ain't nobody." This make me pretty nervous, you know? I mean it really scare me, in a way. There must be three, four hundred people in this room, and I ain't made no speech since my junior year in high school, and I really don't have nothing to say, you understand. When I made that speech in high school, I like to die. They give me this award for setting this attendance record at school. I was there every day for one whole semester, and never late for class. Everybody was there, the principal, the teachers, most of the students, and a bunch of parents. None of my people was there 'cause Moms was in the hospital, Pops was working, and Whodini was in the joint for a breaking and entering. My little sister, Tanya, wasn't there neither, but I didn't give a duck's nuts one way or another about where that heifer was. Last thing I needed was a little squirrel like Tanya up there woofing and carrying on, embarrassing me. The place was crammed with people. They sent me up to the podium to make my speech, but I didn't have nothing to say, right? I mean, what you supposed to say for setting an attendance record? That you just too dumb not to go to school? Or that your mama gave you lotsa Tang and ginger ale?

The whole auditorium was so quiet you couldn't hear nothing but the air conditioners rattling up on the ceiling. When somebody coughed or cleared they throat it sounded like dogs barking. My head was pounding like crazy, and I wondered if the audience could hear it. I cleared my throat and said, "I-I'd like to thank you for this award." But nothing else would come to my mind. Everybody just sat there and waited, but nothing would come to my mind, and I just stood there. The place was quiet as a ninety-year-old widow's bedroom. Then, after a long time, Mr. Grimes, the principal, leapt out his chair and walked over to me, clapping his hands like I done recited the Gettysburg Address backwards in Latin or something. "Thank you very much, Roscoe," he said. Then the audience started clapping along with Mr. Grimes, and I walked off the stage. I just kept on walking, walking, out the door, out the school, and all the way cross town till I got home. Went home, got blazed, and took the bus out to Denver General. Moms was happy to see me, asked me how my speech went.

"OK," I said. "Pop been by?"

Moms tried to laugh, but it didn't sound like no laugh. Sounded like an old car that wouldn't start. "He ain't come by, and he ain't gonna come by. He's ashamed to let these folks see who his wife is."

"Naw, he ain't."

"You know he is too, Ross." She started coughing. Made her body curl up like a fist. Made her eyes water. "He sent his sister over with some of my books —"

"Aunt Shawnette?"

"Who else? Sent her to bring me some of my books and my robe. I asked her when he was gonna come. 'You know I been in the hospital two days,' I said. 'When am I gonna be able to see my husband?' And you know what she said? She said your father's been busy. Said he's been driving O.T. Said he —"

Then she folded her arms across her chest, like she was hugging herself, and cried into the bandage on her right hand. I wanted to cry too, but kept clinching my teeth, inhaling deep and blinking so I wouldn't. Just hugged her while she was hugging herself and told her everything was gonna be fine. When she stopped, I sat down and just stared down at my feet. "Mama," I said, after a while, "I'm quitting school." She just bent up the side of her mouth in that crooked smile of hers.

"I knew it," she said.

"You mad at me?"

"Yeah, I'm mad at you, but what you expect me to do about it with all these tubes and needles in my arms, and me weighing eighty pounds, and one foot, and seven fingers? What you want me to do?"

I reached into my book bag and took out a copy of *The Martian Chronicles*. "I want you to listen," I said, and took her hand. She did. She listened to her blazing son. I read in all kind of voices, voices I never knew was in me. I was There, and There, and There, like my soul was all places, everywhere. And when it was time for me to go she let go of my hand, smiled all crooked at me, and said, "That was beautiful, son. You read so beautiful, baby."

"I don't need school, Mama."

"What do you need, then?"

"Only thing I ever needed," I said back. "I need you." And then I kissed her on her cheek. "Mama?" I said. "Do you feel better? Did the book help?" But she had her eyes closed and said, "Just so beautiful, baby . . . almost There." I looked at her for a while. She didn't look too good. I watched her for a long time. Then when I was sure she was asleep, I split.

Anyway, I never wanted to make no speech in my life, and that's what I tell Melvin, but he just shake his head and say, "Well, there's other places you could hit down here, I guess."

"You mean I can't stay unless I make a speech?"

"Everybody else has. This what you call a collective down here, little brother. You got to freely declare your allegiance to the brothers and sisters. You got to be unified with these people, solidified with 'em. Tell 'em you with 'em all the way, that you'll give it everything you got to keep these folks happy." He fires up another stogie, blows the smoke my way, flicks ashes off his suit. "But you don't got to stay here, man. Take y'time. Look around the place. You got —"

"A speech, huh?"

"Knock it out, blood. Nothing to it."

"All right, Mel, I'll give it my best shot."

"Good, good, good. That's the attitude."

"Just one more thing."

"Mmm."

"What if I can't keep 'em happy?"

Melvin knock his ashes to the floor and chomp the butt between his teeth. "Aw, 'Scoe, man, you worry too much. You can't keep these folks happy it ain't gonna mean it's your fault. It's theirs. And you be free, man, free to choose some other place that suit you." And then he slap me on the back, and it feel creepy, like getting hit with a empty rubber glove. He jump up on one of the desks. I mean he just pop right up there. Look like he still got that forty-eight-inch leap. He pull on his cigar, wave his arms up in the air, and yell, "Yo. Hey,

y'all, listen up. Check this, y'all. Cool!" Everybody gets
real quiet. Somebody turns the stereo way down, and
everybody gathers around me and Melvin. "All right
now, listen. Brother Roscoe here gonna be good enough
to make us his acceptance speech . . ." And someone
say, "Awright!"

"Now, we all know that this party wouldn't have
reached the fever pitch we got now if it wasn't for my
boy, here . . ." And people say, "Uh-huh!" "Yeah!"
"Brother 'Scoe!"

"And I know y'all gonna give him a warm welcome,
just like I know he gonna keep y'all jumping . . ." And
people say, "Owoo!" "Righteous!" "Jumping!"

"So, without further ado, I give you the man of the
hour, the one, the only, Mr. Throw-It-on-Down himself. Ladies and Gentlemen, I give you the Very Large
. . . Mis-tah Roscoe L. Crandel!"

The crowd goes berserk. People throwing confetti,
streamers; they blowing horns, hooting, howling. A
couple a real big dudes steps out the crowd and lifts me
up on the desk next to Melvin. I wave my arms over my
head and they all shut up. Then I clear my throat.

"Ahem," I go like a politician. "Fellow . . . uh,
friends. Thank you . . . Thank you all for the great
evening."

They clap real loud at this, but I wave my arms
again and they shut up like they unplugged.

"Ahem," I say like the last time. "Like, word. I hope
you all having one *hell* of a time."

They go crazy when I say this, and the fat man in the leisure suit laughing so hard, he look like he gonna pop.

"So, let's all have a good time here, and uh . . . damn the torpedoes. For we . . . uh, we all created equal with liberty and whatnot. And I promise you —"

And they applaud some more. Like a whole minute go by before I can shut 'em up.

"And I promise you that it's all for one . . . and one for all. So, peep this. I'll M.C. this thing, like you never seen. So thanks, OK?"

They clapping so hard I can feel the vibrations in my chest. Seem like they never gonna stop. Melvin just standing up on the desk with me, clapping his ass off, puffing on his stogie, and making so much of that blue smoke, I almost can't see him. Then the two big dudes grab me and carry me on they shoulders around the room, so's I can shake folks' hands. The music start back up, and people start cutting up the floor with all these steps I ain't never seen before, and it make me wonder was that blade-face whiteboy playing games on me. But after a minute it occur to me they my steps. My steps. The reason I ain't seen 'em before is 'cause I never seen myself dance. But it's obvious, they done picked up my moves, just like that. The two big dudes put me down, and we do some serious fives and I tell 'em to party till it bleed. They thank me like sons a bitches, like I done saved their lives or something, you dig? And then they shuffle away from me, bowing and scraping like butlers.

The place is busting, and I'm dancing with all kinds a babes, and I jounce 'em every chance I get. I just can't keep a partner for more than twenty minutes. The ones I ain't jounced line up along the side of the table in front of the broom closet, and every once in a while a fight break out if anyone try to cut in line. These hens be illing. I have to go into the men's room every now and then so things can chill. I be hoping they got some 'zines or something for me to read, but they ain't even graffiti on the walls. The bathroom just be full of dudes asking me who I jammed, or do I wanna smoke this or drink that. I can't understand all this. I was never much for the ladies back in the world. Now I ain't saying I was lite. But I always liked having just one squeeze at a time, and I'm pretty shy. I just couldn't make myself say all them smooth words and all them lies just so I could rack up some trim. Danita was my last girlfriend before I died. But in the last few weeks, we wasn't getting along too well. Went with her for eight months, and things were going all right till she got pregnant. She wanted the baby, which was fine by me, but I told her I didn't wanna marry her. Didn't wanna be tied down and strung up. "That's bullshit, girl," I said. But she pretty much cried for three days, and then she got sick, and I felt real bad, so I figured the least I could do was shack with her.

We lived together for about a month, and we got along better than I thought we would. She fixed up my place with pictures on the wall, curtains, plants, silk flowers, peacock feathers, straw fans and wicker, throw rugs and lamps. Crib looked real nice. I'd come from a hard day of peddling the goods at City Park, and the place'd smell like fried chicken or pork chops, spaghetti or something. We'd talk about girls' names and boys' names, and pretty soon, I figured it wouldn't be so bad if we stayed together forever. But that didn't last long. Danita miscarried. To tell you the truth, I didn't even know what a miscarriage was till then. I mean I'd heard the word before, but I really didn't know what it was. And I didn't know it would make me feel so bad either. I felt bad 'cause for a whole month I'd been thinking about what it'd be like to be a pop. I wanted a boy, and I woulda kept him away from ganging, schools, clubs, teams, and speech-making, friend-making. I woulda stopped him from being like Pops and Shawnette, and I sure woulda stopped him from being like Whodini. But Danita'd been doing some thinking too. Told me it was my drug taking that had caused the baby to slip. But I said, "Drugging ain't got nothing to do with nothing, Danita. Why you always on me about that? Why you always looking for an excuse to make me stop? Who put the food on the table? Who pay the rent?"

"You do," she said, and she crossed her bony arms. Her bottom lip started trembling.

I sat down on the couch. "So then —"

"But you don't understand what you doing to yourself," she said. "Don't do nothing but read them damn stupid boring books and smoke that shit and —"

"You said you like me to read to you. You said you like that."

Then she grabbed some of my 'zines off the coffee table and threw 'em in my face. "T' hell with your books, Roscoe! T' hell with 'em! Shouldn't nobody read that much. It ain't right. It ain't normal." I came this close to slapping her upside the head. I didn't, though. I just walked into the bedroom, flamed up the bowl, and when I got greasy high, walked down to Mile High Comics in the cold night and looked through all the sci-fi. Grabbed me a copy of *Brave New World* —which I'd never heard of before — and took the bus to Denver General. Like I say, I was greasy high, high-shine high, high enough to heal Moms, I thought. I was gonna read her a new foot, read her three new fingers, read her fever and pneumonia away. So I got there, and it really surprised me to see all my people there in the hallway outside her room. Shaw-nette was howling and carrying on, saying shit like, "Aw God Lord, she gone. She gone," and clutching her arms around everybody's neck. Pops was telling Shawnette and Tanya to be strong and try to remember the good Moms had in her and all. What the hell did he know about that? Whodini, P-bud, and Sgt. Rex was there too, just standing around in their bad blue clothes; they all had their heads hung down, hands shoved into their pockets. Only one of 'em crying was Rex, which made no sense to me, seeing how he called hisself a hard gangster. I just stood off and watched 'em all, thinking about splitting. Couldn't stand to see all them folks pumping they shoulders up and down, shaking they heads, hugging each other over someone they didn't even know.

Then Shawnette looked up and seen me. "Aw, sugar," she said. "Aw, baby, your mama gone. She gone." She held out her arms to me, the zipper Bible in her left hand. Bitch thought I'd be dumb enough to want to hug her tired red-wig ass. "She gone," she said. I stood there, stuck my hands into my pockets, and just looked at the floor. "Come on over here, boy, and hug your Aunt Shawnie," Pops said. His voice was all mild like, but when I looked up and seen his hard yellow eyes I knew he'da busted my head just as soon as look at me. I didn't move, just stood and looked at him dead in his eye. Everybody was just standing there looking at us. Pops took one step toward me, and just then they wheeled Moms out the room. I walked on by Pops and Shawnette, Whodini, and all the rest, opened up the book to page one, started reading out loud. *A squat grey building of only thirty-four stories . . . all the summer beyond the panes, for all the tropical heat of the room itself . . . a pale corpse-colored rubber. The light was frozen, dead, a ghost . . .* Man I read and read and read and read, till one of the orderlies threw his arm around my shoulder and told me I couldn't go into the morgue with Moms. *Bent over their instruments, three hundred Fertilizers were . . .* Pops caught hold of my arm, but I shook it loose and kept reading. . . . *if they were good and happy members of society*

. . . They closed the elevator door and I kept reading. Loud. Screaming out the words till my throat closed up. Everybody was trying to shush me, put their arms around me, but I just jerked away, croaking out the words. *For in nature it takes thirty years for two hundred eggs to reach maturity* . . . I read, but Mama never got up.

I went home after a long time, after I started crying and couldn't stop, after Whodini busted into some tears and told me I was cutting him too deep. I went home and found Danita'd moved out. Took all her shit. The straw fans, the plants, the silk flowers, the throw rugs. I felt like a fool behind that shit, but it didn't surprise me. Well I guess it did surprise me she'd got her stuff out so clean and fast, but I was expecting her to be gone sooner or later. Never went looking for her either. I went looking for what Moms went looking for. Wasn't nothing to do but stay high, and speak in them voices. I knew I'd find it, maybe more. I wanted to be over it, beyond it, above it.

Anyway, I musta danced with every babe about five or six times by now, and won't be too long till I rearrange every female anatomy in the joint. I'm about as high as I can get. Everything's saying come on, come on, come on, and I've had enough rock to wipe out a hell *full* of Roscoes, but I ain't going down. I'm still standing, still throwing it on down. I just keep getting higher and wider and deeper, and I don't know how long it be before I get There. Seem like a long way off, to tell you the truth. And these people seem to enjoy just about anything I do, but it just make 'em want more. I can't believe the way people listening to me, and laughing at my jokes. They ask me all these heavy intellectual questions, and I be saying anything back and all they do is ooh and aah. Like this brother in a flattop Rise so sharp you could cut your wrist on it say, "Hey, Roscoe, what you think about the South African thing, man?" And I toast up a rock about as big as a knuckle, blow out the smoke. My head sizzling. I say, "It's bullshit, man. It's bullshit." And the brother say back, "Goddamn, man, I just knew it. Wow, yeah. Yeah." And all night long he come back and ask me about Libya, Poland, the Supreme Court, Siskel and that fat dude, it don't matter. I say whatever come to my mind. And they freak.

They look at me like I'm the most important man in hell. And I'd be a lie if I said I didn't like all this. I throw a lamp shade on my head and dance on a desk like you see them cats do in old-time movies, and people laugh till they cry. I do an imitation of John Wayne, once, and some dude say, "Hey, I thought they sent that guy to the other place." Then I start doing requests like Ronald Reagan, Stevie Wonder, Pee Wee Herman, Luther Vandross, Fred G. Sanford, a whole buncha people I never thought I could do at all. But the folks love it, so I do some more. I tell you something about these Hellions. They got a good sense of humor. Damn, I even do my high school principal, Mr.

Grimes, and you just about had to call the paramedics for these people. I tore the roof off the sucker, so to speak. Had 'em rolling. But you can't do nothing twice with these folks, so I keep drinking, keep smoking, so I can come up with something new. Maybe it's a good thing I can't get There as easy as I did back in the world.

A little later, Melvin come up to me all serious like, like somebody'd died or something. Fat chance down here. He walk up to me, with his little stack-a-pancake head all down. His nice little three-piece suit all roughed up, and he ain't even smoking a cigar. This strange, I say to myself, 'cause you never see Melvin without no cigar.

"Hey, little brother," Melvin say.

"Whassamatter, Melmac?"

"I'm afraid it's time for us to go our separate ways, my man."

"Wha— how come? Am I boring you?"

"What? What? The Master of Space Out and Good Time? Who you kidding, brother? Naw, look here, man, it's like I got a job to do. Got to sweep up the foyer, get the paperwork ready for the next guests, show folks around, order shit for the front desk. It's not just a job, Jackson, it's hell. So. You all set? Everything cool?"

"It's clean, Melvundo. It's tasty. Don't worry. I'm happy."

"Good. All you gotta do" — and he whip out some

papers from his pocket — "is sign these, right here and right there. Here's a pen. You sure you wanna be here, now?"

"You know a better place?"

"Prob'ly not, homes. Not for you, anyway."

"Well, Mel, catch you on the bound, man."

"Keep 'em happy, little brother. Easy up."

"Say, Mel? One thing, homes."

"Talk to me." Then Mel fire up a stog and blow smoke my way.

"Like, you said one time that everybody end up in hell, right?"

"That's right. Everybody."

"You get to meet almost everybody down here, right?"

"Not almost. Everybody. Period."

"Well, dig, man, you ever seen my moms?"

"Sure, brother. Nice lady. She was real happy about having her fingers and foot back. Why you ask?"

I cock my head and just look at him for a minute. What he mean, Why I'm asking about her? "Just seem to me this be the kind of place she might like to be. That's all."

Melvin throw up his hands and say, "She did, for a while, brother. Easy up, man."

"Mel, wait up."

He throw his arms up in the air, drops his head, sighs. "Look, little brother. She couldn't make it, OK? The broad spent all her time talking about books. I'm saying books. These folks ain't got no use for that. She was assigned someplace else and don't ask me where. Ain't my job to know. And don't ask me can you go see her, 'cause you cain't, even if I knew. And get off that My-Momma-and-Her-Sweet-Self booj-wah, hank-chief-head, cliché doodah, doodah bu'shit. Ain't no such thing as a self, for one thing, homejames. And for another thing . . ." He grinning now. "Every-body's happy down here. Awright? Now. Any more questions?"

"Just one."

"Speak."

"Some babe here was talking like I was supposed to be here, like this whole gig is for me. I just wanna know what —"

He holds both his palms up in my face. "It is for you," he say, "till you cain't handle it no more. You cain't handle it, somebody else will. Now, if you don't mind —"

"Why?"

"Say what?"

"Why am I here?"

Melvin snap his cigar out his mouth, drop it, step on it, and fold his arms behind his back. He just stand there, looking at the ground like he thinking real hard. Then he grab another cigar out his jacket, flame it up, and say, "Look here, boy. Like I tell you, everybody go to hell." He struts away like a black Slinky with feet, and disappears through the wall.

I stand there for a long time and don't say nothing or do nothing. I just stare at the place I seen ol' Melvin walk through. And for the first time, I stop and really ask myself just what the fuck I'm doing here. It don't make no sense. I mean, there I was, looking down at all them hospital folks in their white coats running around, telling me to come on, come on, come on, telling me I was too young. Sheeit, what do they know? They didn't know nothing about the sweet rock that make you float so good, that make you own the world, but not able to change the world, that lock up your lungs and make your heart purr like a cat instead of beat. And they might know the rock can kill you, if you not careful, but they sure as hell don't know about you slipping from your body like a silent fart, and how you be floating the fuck away from your mighty-righteous aunt, your proud sober daddy, your jive-ass friends and they so-called gang, your straight semesters in high school, your disappearing girlfriend, your shyness, your dullness, your book reading, and your own damn self so you can find out where your mama went. And what they know about bouncing and jouncing and ouncing, and being here? The women fine, and the dudes treat me like I know my bidness. Which I do. I keep 'em happy. I got to keep 'em happy. I work my ass off keeping 'em happy. All these down partiers, all this grub, all these jams, the flashing lights, the liquor, the three-piece suits, the herbs, the rock. There's enough to keep this crowd cranked up forever. Really. Forever. I'm here, getting higher and funnier, and louder and longer, and faster, and deeper, and kinkier, and drunker, funkier, and believe me you, buh-boy, it's a long, long way from here to There. It's a long, long way.

Peacetime

/ / / / / /

It was a pretty weird time. Little Martinez was dead, and so was Zoot the Boot. Little Martinez got drunk when his fiancée pink-slipped him for some long-haired dude, and so driving on some highway in Texas, drunk like he was, he stopped his car — just like that — got out, and started directing traffic. They say when they found him he'd been run over four or five times. Guy's head was about as thick as a T-bone steak, they say. And like Zoot had been shot right between the eyes by some gang dude in East L.A. Zoot'd gone home for the weekend. Corporal Ski and PFC Mike O.D.'d on angel dust. Lopez was dead and Forehead was dead. Car wreck. Bob the Hick was dead. Wife capped his ass with his forty-five. Sergeant Eyeball was dead. Suicide. Got busted to PFC for stealing a guy's radio. Couldn't hack the pay cut, I guess. Anyway, all these dudes were dead as fuck. It kind of made you wish there'd been a war so at least some of these guys could have had some decent memorial services and made their families some insurance cash. But most of 'em had been on unauthorized absences — U.A., we used to call it — when they'd got iced. The rest'd died drugging or stealing shit, or, like Bob the Hick, after beating their old ladies one too many times. Like that. You wished there'd been a war to give these guys something to do, too.

I almost took the big chill myself when Barney and Long Tall took me to get laid for my first time. Up in East L.A., where Barney's girlfriend lived. This was in 1973, during the year the U.S. pretty much completed its pullout, and when just about everybody had a bad attitude about guys in the military. This includes guys in the military. You'd say to a guy, "What's happenin, Marine?" and he'd say, "I ain't no damn Marine, I'm a future ex-Marine." We used to say things like, "Eat the apple and fuck the Corps," and we used to say USMC stood for Uncle Sam's Maroon Crotch. Saying morale was low was like saying Abraham Lincoln's a little dead. The Corps was letting in guys who couldn't read, guys who had needle tracks up and down their arms. Sometimes a judge would tell a young guy, "Awright, buddy, two years in jail or four years in the Corps," and the Corps'd take 'em.

And as for civilians, I don't know how many long-haired types'd throw me the finger or moon me out the window of a speeding van while I'd just be hanging out in Oceanside. I mean, I wasn't exactly the kind of guy who wore "high-n-tight" haircuts and tattoos that read Yuck Fou or DEATH BEFORE DISHONOR. Hell no. My mustache was always too bushy to make regulation, hair was too long. But it wasn't just hair, it was me. I read novels, didn't drink, practiced T.M., played the flute, and had never had a fight in my life. I was mellow. You know, one of them sensitive motherfuckers. And like I said, I was a virgin. You'd think a guy like me wouldn't even join the Corps in the first place, but there was this bad week I had, see, when I got fired from my job at Safeway for sleeping in the bathroom while I was supposed to be buffing the floors. Well, on the way home from work that day my '65 Mustang — great car — broke down and I ended up looking at five hundred bills worth of repairs; then Jeanette, this beautiful college woman I was seeing, sacked me for reasons that still ain't clear to me today. Prob'ly 'cause I was a virgin. I joined because it was the quickest way out of town. I didn't want to be sent off to Viet Nam, which at the time was about as likely to happen as being sent to New Brunswick. Actually, I wanted to play the flute in the Marine Corps band. What else could I do? I wanted out of town and I played the flute. To my eighteen-year-old brain it was perfect — "Flautist? Join the Marines! Get out of town!" See, I'd quit high school at seventeen to work full-time at Safeway, so college was the furthest thing from my mind. I hated school. But maybe if I'd stayed in school I'd've been smart enough to think of things like Junior College; the Employment Office;

Buy a New Car, Stupid. Shoot, never even got to
audition for the band. Instead, they made me a radio
operator and stuck me in the First Reconnaissance Bat-
talion. If I'd known they were gonna do me like that
I'da stayed home, got a job at a fast-food place or
something.

And if I'd known that joining the Crotch was gonna
make it so hard to get laid, and that getting laid for the
first time was gonna just about get me killed, well . . . It
was like this: The kind of girls who'd pay you two
seconds of attention, if you were a Marine, were mostly
the same kind who go for serial killers and pimps. Now
for a lot of jarheads this is perfect. Lotta those guys
want babes who're amused by tattoos and jackboots.
I'm sure I ain't got to explain the whys and wherefores a
that nonsense. But let's face it. What choice did some of
us guys have? We weren't bankers. We weren't heroes.
What were we? We were REMFs, man: rear-echelon
mother— and you know the rest. What kinda seventies
woman'd wanna get serious about a guy whose job it is
to patrol through California sheep pastures, keep his
hair short, take rifles and radios apart just to put 'em
back together? I mean, you're at some civilian club with
a date, right? And this guy with a chin like a ham, and
hair out to here and a nine-million-dollar disco suit
walks up to her when you go to take a leak, and the guy
says, "Hey there, my name's Rusty. Banker-slash-
Playboy. So, who's the short-haired dude you're with?
Private Nerf, eh? Cool name. What's he do? Hmm,

interesting. You say he dive-bombs on cigarette butts, swabs decks, paints rocks, sleeps on something called a fart sack, and says fucken this and fucken that every three seconds? What is he" — and he's sniggering now, this guy — "a Mah-reeeen?"

So you start taking your dates to the enlisted men's club on base, right? And in less time it takes the suds on your beer to fizz away you'd be surrounded by about fifty ka-billion pinhead lance corporals yacking about how drunk they'd been when they smoked down some frontage road at mach twenty-six on the night before they reported to boot camp. "Yeah, dude, I got what you might call a speed complex er some shit. Hell, I was even wilder back then than I am now. My fucken hair was down ta fucken here, and my Camaro had a Hunkman shifter, a number-six hemi-plotus wheel and three hundrit thirty-three pounds scrunch power per cubic inch, man." And the crummy thing for a basically boring guy like me was that your date would usually end up being more interested in one of these weasel penises than you before two hours'd gone by.

I make it sound like this kind of thing happened to me all the time, but that's not so. Actually, I only had two dates when I was in the Crotch. Two dates. Two women. You know, it's funny. I hadn't intended to let my virginity go on for so long. I thought for sure I'd've lost it by then. Before I'd enlisted, I'd thought of sex as more or less standard military issue. You know: *One pack, Federal Stock Number 03395N-dash-1; two pair size-*

thirteen combat boots, FSN 44659T-dash-1; one mysterious, dark, voluptuous woman, FSN 382436-dash-1. "This woman is your best friend, Marine. Keep her clean, learn how to dress her and undress her blindfolded. You take care a her and she'll take care a you." Things just didn't go the way I thought they would. Maybe I respected those two women, maybe I was afraid. I don't remember anymore. And I couldn't see paying for sex. Too many of my buddies came back to the squad bay with lice, recurring sores; too many of them had homely, overweight girlfriends who made them miserable or stole from them. If it'd been 1943 instead of 1973, it might have been easier on a lot of us. Those babes woulda stood outside the squad bay on those Friday afternoons in their long shirts and bobby socks, or whatever, standing on their toes, holding their purses up against their boobs, burning like a hunka hunka burning love. But in those days our hair was too short, our faces too naked, our politics totally "noncorrectional," as we used to say. That's why I turned to Barney and Long Tall, I guess.

Long Tall was this dark, dark, dark-skinned brother from Wisconsin. Nice dresser, Long Tall was, but he had his own style: creased jeans, jersey, T-shirt, Hush Puppies, vest; his hair was always pomaded, patted, parted; his mustache razored neat as a painted-on eyebrow. I always dug that guy, admired him, you could say, for never believing much of what the Corps tried to pound into us. He'd split from camp whenever he was so moved, came back when he felt like it. The funny thing was that neither the first sergeant, Sergeant Dark, nor the company commander — this little Annapolis twit we called Super Chicken — ever really insisted on punishing him much for going U.A. But after three years in the Crotch he'd never gone any higher in rank than private first class, and most of the time he stayed at private. But he had this kind of magic. You just couldn't dislike him. Even serious Necks liked him.

This guy was something else. He was great at card tricks, and he liked to spit lighter fluid on lighter flames to make these, like, great big fire balloons. Kafwoom! Guy was nuts. He liked to stay high, do handstands, sleep late. His job was what we called police sergeant, which, believe me, ain't got jack to do with law and order. Just order. See, "policing" is a military term for janitor work, OK? So, Long Tall picked up trash, cleaned toilets, swabbed decks, polished doorknobs. Super Chicken gave him the job after the third or fourth time he'd gone U.A. He wanted to keep an eye on him, or something. Long Tall loved it, see, 'cause he had the freedom to work at his own pace, set pretty much his own hours. He even moved his wall locker and rack into this giant supply closet, just down the hall from the squad bay.

See, a "squad bay" is what the army calls a barracks, OK?

Well, anyhow, Long Tall never, like, snuck away

when he'd decide it was time to split, in fact he'd leave a note on First Sergeant Dark's door before he'd split. Sergeant Lopez asked Long Tall just a couple days before Lopez croaked himself in a car wreck in San Clemente, he said, "How the fock do you get off just taking these little vacations, vato?" And ol' Long Tall just smiled, pulled this rabbit's foot key chain from his pocket, waved it in front of Lopez's face, and said, "I just hypmotize anybody who get in my way." I think Lopez believed him, too. I know I did.

This other guy, Barney — he was from Utah, I think — was Long Tall's best bud. Barney had his own kind of magic, too, but it was a little scarier. It's hard to explain how, though, because Barney wasn't a big guy, and I never saw him hurt anybody but himself. He smoked a lot of angel dust, see, and it made him do strange stuff. Sometimes it was funny, like the time he got naked, spray painted his hairy ol' chest with a big "B" and went running out the squad bay and into the street. Yeah, he did. A bunch of us followed him out there. He just stood out in the street, holding up his right hand to stop cars. Stopped a bunch of 'em, too. Then, when it looked like a few pissed off Marines were gonna get out of their cars and stomp Barney's face, Barney went running off down the road with his left arm pointing to seven o'clock and his right shooting up at two o'clock. We watched him till he was up and over the hill. What I thought was so funny and weird about it was that Barney never said a word the whole time.

Not one word. He didn't make super-hero music or flying sounds either. Nothing.

But like I'm saying, man, is that the guy was scary. If you knew the guy, you just sensed it. You heard him use those . . . what I used to think was . . . big words, and you heard him talk about his two and a half tours to Viet Nam. You saw the guy just, I don't know, do something flaky like braid his chest hairs or walk around in his goddamn olive-drab utility jacket, a paisley tie, skivvies, and a blond wig . . . and he's just stretching out on his rack, reading the *Paris Review.* Something tells you not to mess with a guy like that. But a guy who didn't know him and messed with him would get a real nice surprise like the motor pool gunny sergeant who was acting officer of the day. You know, the guy who goes around checking out the guards and the armory, supply and, like, is responsible for reveille. Well, this gunny sergeant struts into the squad bay at "oh-dark-thirty" in the morning, flips on the lights, and like usual, we got up. But Barney didn't. This wasn't unusual for him, and ninety-nine times out of a hundred, people'd just let him be. But this gunny, well . . .

He strutted up to Barney's rack and tapped Barney in the ribs with the toe of his patent leather shoe and said, "Hey, M'rine, git yer ass up." Barney don't budge, right? And the guy poked Barn with his nightstick, OK? And he said, "Hey, son, you got five minutes ago to git yer ass up. You want me to write you up? 'Cause I'd be more'n —" And KaFloom! Barney leaped up from bed like a wet cat and pushed his rack over, and just like dominoes, rack, wall locker, rack, wall locker, rack, wall locker go tumbling down. And Barney says, "You wanna fuck with me? You wanna write me up? You wanna fuck with me? You wanna write me up? Come on, motherfucker, write me up. I got something for your ass!" The gunny's so freaked that you could practically see the exclamation points and cartoon sweat flying from his forehead. Holy Jesus. But Barney wasn't done. He spun around and started punching out windows, ka-ting! ka-ting! ka-bing! Blood's all over the place, glass's all over. And then I walked up to Barney. I don't know why I did, and if I hadn't Barney and I and Long Tall might never've become friends and I wouldn't have started running around East L.A. with these guys and doing the idiot shit they did, and then with a brain full of angel dust and weed one night, admit to these guys I was a virgin, then let them talk me into going to that party in East L.A. . . . well, I'll get to that in a sec.

See, I hardly knew Barney. Our entire — what you could call — association was that his rack was across the squad bay from mine and I watched his antics when I was broke and there wasn't much else to do. Every great once in a while I'd lend him something I'd read or he'd do the same for me, but we didn't really talk a lot. Sometimes we played pool. But we weren't friends. So why I walked over to his bloody ass and put my hand on his shoulder while his back was to me and he was fixing to punch window number six or seven, I don't know. And why I knew exactly what to say to him while he was so pumped up to take lives, I don't know. But I said to him, "Hey, Barney, man, cut it out. You're bleeding." And why he didn't spin around and split my lip or leap into my mouth and toss my entrails out my ears, I don't know. And why he just said, "Good point, Bones," I just plain don't know. But that's what I did and that's what I said; and that's what he did and that's what he said. The gunny's ears were red and his bottom lip was wet and trembling and white. He said, "Y-you b-better do something with that crazy bastard. Y-you better get him outta my sight!" I wrapped Barn's arm in a couple towels and walked him to the infirmary. All the way there Barney kept saying, "You know, Bones, sometimes I think I'm crazy. You think I'm crazy?" He said this two or three times, and all I could say back every time was, "Naw, man, you're just smart and frustrated. You shouldn't have to be sitting around in a goddamn Marine Corps radio shack swatting flies and sweeping floors. You're just frustrated."

So the three of us just started hanging out together. The Corps is like that. It ain't like in the civilian world, where you drive home to your place, and I drive home to mine, and we only see each other for eight or nine hours a day. No, no, no. Married guys could do that. And some of the gay guys lived off base, and a few others, too, but most of us lived in these big squad bays. No separate rooms, no private showers. Hell, in some of the places we were stationed, they didn't even build stalls around the crappers. I'm not kidding, man, when we were at Camp Tulega I didn't go to the bathroom for a week. And for months I'd get up at three A.M. to do my stuff.

But it's weird. One guy's in the corner playing Barry White, and the guy across from him's playing Tom T. Hall. Bailey's jamming to his reggae; Grapehead's blasting Supertramp; Martinez is digging Malo; Bones has got his earphones on and his flute to his lips and he's trying to keep up with Yusef Lateef, and can't. Gregoire, Long Tall, Williams, Forehead, and Busey are playing craps in some other corner, and in the opposite corner, Big J. from L.A., 'Orporal 'Ump, Little Martinez, and Stevie are studying the Bible. The Slope is in his rack, pretending to be asleep, but everybody knows he's spanking the monkey. There we were, seventy-five guys doing fifty different things, and ninety percent of the time it worked. And you find that everybody's interesting. Just about everybody has a story to tell, and even though you find yourself getting sick of guys who drive "rilly fucken fast," and the guys who borrow your stuff and sell it or lose it. Even though you know that ninety-nine percent of these buttheads would sooner hang by their tongues on meat hooks than let you marry their sisters, and that most'd forget your name if they didn't see you for forty-eight hours, you still find yourself really wanting to listen to them. And even more than that, man, you find yourself, one night, sitting in a big old drainpipe about two hundred yards from the beach, smoking joints laced with PCP, even though you've never smoked before. You find you're with Barney and Long Tall and you're hearing this deep echoey voice saying, "Well you guys are lucky even if you can't see your women every night. I've never slept with a woman."

"Get outta here, man," Long Tall said.

"I figured as much," Barney said. "You're too easy-going." And when they both just sort of said, "Hm . . . hm," you had to know what they were thinking. Except I didn't know anything. I was too ripped. Barney looked like a hairy little duck. Ed looked like a weasel. It felt as though we were zooming through space in a rocket, and something made me say "oooOOOooo!" — what I guess I thought was some kinda science fiction music. But just like it was on cue, Barney and Long Tall started singing, "Love jooooones! I gotta love joo-ooones! I gotta love jones, babeh, babeh, oo-oOOOooo!" When our ship landed, we walked back to the squad bay with our arms, you know, over each other's shoulders, singing, "We Gotta Get You a Woman."

So the next weekend, see, we climbed into Barn's V.W. Bus, cranked down the windows, smoked this and that, drank this and that, and headed for Barney's girlfriend's apartment in East L.A. July was her name. The only person I knew who'd met July was Long Tall, but I'd heard a lot about her, and Barney confirmed a

lot of the stuff I thought was all bull. Like that she was a
ballerina, a waitress, and a tightrope walker. How she
got to be all these things I didn't ask, but I did learn that
mainly she was a waitress in a heavy-metal bar in Hollywood. "How'd you meet her?" I asked Barney. I said
this while I was looking at all the cars on the highway,
checking out the Pacific Ocean, bopping my head to
Barney's Bachman/Turner Overdrive tape — "Takin
care o' business. We be takin care o' business." I felt I
was being extremely cool for a dude who was purposely
driving up Highway One-oh-one with a couple of guys
who'd practically guaranteed me my manhood. Barney
said, "Me and L.T. go up to Hollywood a lot. I prob'ly
met her at the bar she works at." I thought that was a
pretty bizarre answer, but I didn't say anything. But
then Long Tall goes, "Heh-heh-heh." And he said,
"The past is in the past. Heh-heh-heh."

Then Barney said, "Fucken 'A.' 'That was yesterday
and yesterday's gone.' "

And Long Tall said, "Veee-Eht Nam! Kills
mem'ries dead."

"You got a problem with that, black man?"

"Not me, Messican."

"Indian!"

"Sheeit."

"I am! I ain't no fucken Chicano. I'm a fucken
Hopi."

"You're Indian?" I said.

"Yeah, he is, but I like to give him a hard time. Heh.

July know he Indian, too, but her folks don't. If they did, they'd prob'ly bushwhack his ass."

Barney lifted both hands from the wheel and bounced his fingertips off his chest, boink, boink, boink. I put my eyes on the road and dug my foot into the floorboard. "I got something for their asses if they fuck with me," Barn said. And I said, "What. You gonna breast-feed 'em?" I didn't take my eyes off the road, like I say, but I could tell he'd put his hands back on the wheel from the way the bus swerved straight. Long Tall chuckled, but Barney flattened his lips to-gether and shook his head. "More like chest-feed 'em," he said. "Should I show 'im, L.T.?"

I could tell Long Tall was joking when he said, "Don't do it, Barn. Don't do it."

"It's too late, Robin. I must. Can't seem to con-trol s-self. I must." He leaned close to me, right? And he popped open the glove box and yanked out his sun-glasses and his motor cap, slapped 'em on, and looked at me. Then he jerked his head back and looked at Long Tall. Then he snapped his head to the left and looked out the driver-side window. It was funny, but there was this, like, weird edge to it too. I started feeling like I was back in that tunnel, flying through space. Oo-oOOOooo. But to tell you the truth I wasn't all that surprised when Barney pulled the pistol from inside his jean jacket. Figures, I thought. He's gonna shoot us all. Yep. He's got this stupid nickel-plated thirty-eight and he's gonna do us and then we'll all be dead. Yep. "L.T.'s got one, too," he said. "We never told you about 'em before 'cause we weren't sure about you."

Long Tall said, "Yeah, main, you need one where we be going sometimes." I'm thinking, Well, where in the name a God be we going, dude? But I didn't say anything, and neither did anyone else for a while. Cars rolled by us and we rolled by cars: purple, silver, green, red, red, red, blue. I was just checking out the colors of all the cars I saw. Long Tall lit a cigarette, and Barney pulled his motor cap off and slid the gun back inside his coat. Then Barn said, "My mother's Indian and my father's Jewish. July's people — ah, her real name's Juanita . . . Archuleta — well her people really don't like me, but we never see 'em, and if we did, they wouldn't do anything. Don't worry."

We got hungry from smoking all that pot and — no angel dust this time. No, that was the first and last time I'd tried it, that once. Bad stuff.

So we were hungry, like I'm saying, and as soon as we got to L.A. we pulled into a Kentucky Fried and got one of those nine-million-piece buckets. We bought some more beer and packed off to Balboa Park. Now that was great. Gorgeous women were everywhere. It was, like, tube tops and shorts and bikini tops and shorts and halter tops and shorts. All these Chicano women. Yeah, they're nice, ain't they? And about fifty yards away from us there was this group of percussionists: timbales and bongos and congas and sticks, whistles, maracas, and all just wailing away on this bad-ass salsa jam. We were all just sitting around, looking and listening, chowing down, cooking under the sun, cooling under the breeze. And then this red Frisbee zipped in and knocked over Long Tall's malt liquor. "Hey, sorry, vato," this guy said, and he ran up, bent over, and stood up Long Tall's can. From the second I saw this guy, I tell you, man, I did not like him.

He was slick looking, handsome, nice long black hair, political smile, jeans creased sharp enough to shave a Georgia peach. If it wasn't for the fact he had these two homemade tattoos on his wrists, a lightning bolt and a cross on one arm and this blotchy-looking I-don't-know-what on the other arm, I woulda thought he was an actor or something. "No big thing," said Long Tall. He picked up his beer and took a swig. He stretched out on the grass and leaned back on his elbows. "Wanna brewski?" he said to the guy. "Yeah, man, thanks," the guy said back and snatched one up, cracked it open, and sat cross-legged next to Barney. Then this slick guy said, "Hey, you guys are in the Marines, right?"

"Nope," said Barney. "Cowboys."

The guy laughed. Long Tall just kinda grinned. I just gave the guy the fish eye. He wasn't paying me any mind anyway. While he was laughing — a little too loud and long, I figured — he was eyeballing our bucket of bird. "Chow down," I said. So we all four sat there, listening to the jams and drinking and grubbing. In no time it was like he and Barney were best buds. They were smacking palms and patting each other's backs, and calling each other homey and cousin. This made me mistrust this guy even more. He was just too goddamn nice. The guy kept asking us the usual questions: Joo guys fight in Nam? Do they really make you guys beat each other up when you graduate from boot camp? Hey, how come you guys gotta cut your hair like that? C'n you really kill a guy in seven seconds? Really? Ay chi-wow, vato, that's cool. Then he asked what we were doing here, and before either of my friends could say anything, I said, "Just looking to party."

"I know where there's gonna be a great party at," the dude said. And the next thing you know, we're blowing down the freeway, following the guy's metallic lime green V.W. Beetle as it zipped and swerved in and out of traffic. I thought my heart was gonna bust. I wanted to tell Barney to slow down, cool out, forget this guy; he gives me the major hoodads. Hey, gotdammit, slow the hell down. Instead I said, trying to not sound anxious, "So, we still gonna check out your girlfriend's place?"

Barney grinned. "Say, L.T., you hear this guy? He wants some groin cakes and he wants 'em now."

Long Tall's just going "Heh-heh-heh," real slow.

"No it ain't that," I said. "I just —" But Barney slugged me on the arm and said, "Don't worry, Bones, everything's already set up for tonight. July's got this friend, Carlotta's her name. Carly's damn fine and likes to ball brothers. L.T.'s poked her innumerable times. Right, Tall One?"

"Heh-heh-heh."

"Just kidding, Bones. She likes soul brothers, but L.T.'s never balled her."

"Not when I can trim your girlfriend," Long Tall said.

Barney grinned and shook his head, but said, "Carly's a stripper, but she's smart as hell and hasn't had a boyfriend for 'bout six months. Makes good money, too. Hey, L.T., gimme a beer." Barney popped that beer open and tipped his head back, swigging. "Hey, watch the road," I said. And Barney said back, "What we were gonna do was hang out in Hollyweird for a few hours, see some fuck flicks, maybe intimidate a few queers. Yeah, we like to come up here and stand on the street corners, going" — and he started up with the boink, boink, boink on his chest — " 'Hey, queer bait, come here. I got something for you to suck.' " Long Tall leaned forward and dropped his hand onto my shoulder. "You need a piece, I know where I could get one for you. Only cost you twenty, thirty bucks."

And Barney said, "No time for that, L.T., we're partying tonight."

In no time we were pulling up to this ranch-style house in the burbs just outside East L.A. Our cheesy host brought us some beer, and we sat in his living room drinking away. I couldn't stand the taste of beer then, so I was doing about a half can for every two or three the other guys were quaffing. Actually, the place was pretty nice. Fifty ka-billion potted plants, macramé all over. A big orange, brown, and white God's eye hanging behind the couch. New-looking couch, too, I remember. There was this velvet painting of a caballero on horseback. I guess now I think those things are pretty tacky, but it looked OK hanging in this guy's house. It was a nice, hip sixties/seventies Chicano hippie's pad, whatever that means.

Then the guy — his name was Eddie, I believe — Eddie said, "You guys wanna meet my honey?"

We all either shrugged, nodded, or both, and Eddie stood up and led us outside. He stopped in front of the garage and just stood there for a minute, grinning at us real funny. I have no idea how my two partners felt, but I was having serious hoodads about this guy. Oo-oOOOooo! Finally, the guy yanked up the garage door — that was one clean garage, man, nothing outta place — and walked to this motorcycle that was covered with a tarp. You could tell from the tires it was a hog. He slid back the tarp like you'd slide a bra off a breast. It was a pretty bike: enough chrome and glitter to make a three-star general jealous, and the tank was metallic blue in a kind of starburst pattern. But nice as it was there was no reason for Eddie to start rubbing his crotch like he did. Yeah, he did, but that's nothing compared to what he did after that.

OK, he's rubbing his crotch, right? He's saying, "Ain't she sweet? Ain't she sexy? Her name's Rosita."

And then he lies over the bike and starts humping the seat, and rubbing the gas tank. That long hair of his kind of fell over his face, so you couldn't see exactly, but I'm pretty sure he was kissing the top of the tank. He kept saying, "I love you, love you, love you," over and over. Then he pretended to shoot his load, then went limp and plopped to the floor. After a second he grabbed the bike's footrest and said, "Was it good for you?" This made Long Tall and Barney crack up, but I started feeling sick, like. I wanted to get out of there. I started thinking about telling Barney to just take me the hell to a bus station or something. I didn't like this guy one bit. And this is where it gets even weirder.

We went back into the house, see, and the second I walked into the house I was just about knocked flat by the sight of this woman in this electric wheelchair. She sure as hell hadn't been there before, but there she was, sitting right there in the middle of the living room. I tried not to stare, but I couldn't help it. She had little baby legs and arms, but a big body. A big head, too. I mean bigger than normal, almost like the head of a pro linebacker on the head of a normal-sized woman. No, I'm not exaggerating, either, and I'm not trying to be funny. She just . . . her eyes bulged and her teeth were so bucked she couldn't close her mouth. She had a big square jaw, about the size of a guy's wallet, maybe. But she had a beautiful voice. Her voice sounded like a French horn when she spoke, but she spoke in Spanish so I didn't have any idea what she was saying. Eddie

answered her in English: "I know, *hermanita*, I will.
Don't you worry now, everything's cool." And then he
turned half right and winked at Barney. Barney nodded
like he knew what Eddie's little sister had said. Eddie
rested his hands on the armrests of the wheelchair and
kissed the woman's forehead.

Maybe I'll seem a little twisted for saying this, but,
well . . . see, I was feeling paranoid and weird and my
thoughts were just tumbling a mile a second and I
found myself thinking that maybe Carly, the woman I
was supposed to meet that night, looked like this
woman in the wheelchair. And I was trying to wipe
outta my head the thought of what it'd be like to kiss
those teeth and undress her, and you know. Then I
started thinking even loonier crap like how maybe Eddie would climb into his sister's bed and dry-hump her
like he'd done to the Harley. I think I was just too faced.
I just wanted to go home, back to the base. It was
starting to get dark outside, and everything was too
quiet, too . . . something. Finally Eddie said, "Let's go,
guys. Follow me in your ride. We gotta go by my
buddy's place and pick up some herb. You guys do
herb?"

So by the time we got to this other guy's house, it
was dark, city dark, with yellow and pink street-lamp
lights mixed around with the night. We pulled up to the
place. It was another suburban-style place, with neat
hedges and lawns. We'd had to park a ways away from
the house because of all the cars in front of the house.

Looked like a party. When we got out of the bus, Eddie jogged up to us and said, "You guys just hang out here. Mike don't like strangers hanging around his place. Be back in a minute." Then he jogged off. He went into the house and then I noticed that a bunch of dudes were hanging out in the front yard of the place. They were about a good twenty yards from us. They were swigging beer; their cigarette cherries were floating through space like giant lightning bugs. I couldn't tell exactly how many of them there were. It was like this tangle of silhouettes painted on velvet in, you know, a darker kind of black. I knew they were checking us out, sizing us up. The screen door slapped shut and I turned to look at Eddie walking down the steps of the porch. Instead of coming our way, he walked to the group of dudes, and you could tell that they were whispering to each other.

Then Eddie went back into the house. Then he went back out and talked to the guys. Then he went back inside. He did this a couple more times and I could almost hear them saying, Yeah, let's get our motorcycle chains and crack these guys' skulls and take their money. I was nervous as hell. Long Tall lit up a cigarette, and I realized I'd forgotten my friends were there. So I said to both of 'em, "What time'd you say we're supposed to meet July?"

"Fucken Bones wants that leg bad, Barn."

"What're you worried about, Bones? We got all weekend. Listen, we'll just go by July's place when we leave the party, OK? They'll be there. Anyway, it's just up the road. Won't take long to get there at all."

"It ain't that," I said. "It's just that I don't trust these guys."

"Whassa matter," Long Tall said, "you scared a Mexicans?"

Barney said, "Yeah, what's your problem, Bones, you racist?"

I stuffed my hands into my pockets and I said, "Look, do you know these guys? You don't know these guys. What's taking Eddie so damn long? Why's he keep going in and outta the house like that?"

And Barney said, "Looks like to me he's collecting a few alms so he can buy the herb." Then he fired up his own smoke, folded his arms, and leaned against the car. At that second a cop car pulled up. Two big blond cops got out the car and one of 'em just stood by the car and the other one walked up to us. He wasn't wearing a hat, and I could see from the headlights that were shining on us that his gun holster was unsnapped. "Good evening, gentlemen," the cop said.

"What's the problem, officer?" Barney said, and I held my breath, thinking he'd start up with the boink, boink, boink on his chest, pull out his thirty-eight, and get us all shot to pieces. But he didn't get weird. Barney could be very cool at times. The cop said, "Listen, we got a complaint about a group of people in the neighborhood getting rowdy, drinking beer, and tossing their cans on the ground. This is a quiet neighborhood.

They don't like that sort of thing." He was big and pink, with a flat nose. He looked like he could hurt a guy.

"Ain't us," said Long Tall. The cop didn't say anything to us. He just flashed his light into our eyes to see how ripped we were, then flashed his light into Barney's bus. Without one word the cop opened up the passenger-side door, opened the glove box, and started rifling through it. I could see him take something from the box and place it on the seat. "Pig just found my herb, L.T.," said Barney. Then the cop looked under the seats, and pulled something from under it. Next he got out the bus, went to the front of it, and opened up the trunk. "Aw, Jesus," said Barney, "I got some speed in the — too late." After a couple of minutes, the cop stepped up to us and said, "You guys from Camp Pendleton?" He had the pot, the speed, and a bandolier from an M60 machine gun. "Yes sir," said Barney. "We're United States Marines."

"I thought so," the cop said. "You got a lot of stuff here I think your first sergeant wouldn't approve of. But instead of locking you up, I'm just gonna ask you to leave East L.A."

I was standing there thinking, Thank you God.

"What about them guys?" Barney said.

"Never mind," Long Tall told him.

"I'm giving you about two minutes," said the cop. "Get gone and stay gone. Don't you worry about those guys; they're next." And then he walked away. We got into the bus. The screen door of the house swung open and Eddie yelled, "Hey, where you guys going?"

"Where's the party at?" said Long Tall.

And the guy yelled out 419 such and such a street. "You know how to get there?"

"No prob," said Barney.

"Barney," I said.

He knew what I was gonna say, I guess, because he turned real fast and looked at me. "You think those cops are gonna follow us all the fuck over East L.A.?" he said. "Grow up, man!" Then he cranked up the bus and yelled out the window, "See you there, Eddie!"

So Barney peeled outta there, like there weren't any cops around. We got to the other neighborhood in ten, fifteen minutes. I was actually starting to feel all right for some reason. I don't know, there was this cool air blowing in the window, and there was this cool jam by War popping out the radio. You know, "Low-ri-der don't use much gas, now . . . Low-ri-der don't drive too fast." Something like that, anyway, something by War. Man, I'm getting old, can't even remember. But like I'm saying, I was feeling OK. I figured, Look, no way is this guy gonna take you to a bus station, Boneyboy, so you mize well lay on back an' roll wit' it. That's just what I was thinking. It was pretty dark and we were slow rolling along the streets, stopping every so often, Barney, like, craning his neck out the window. "OK, here we go," he said. "Four-eleven, four-thirteen, four-fifteen, seventeen . . . what the . . ." He went just like that, he went, "What the . . ." And Long Tall said, "Hey, main, look like it ain't no four-nineteen."

"Looks like it," Barney said.

And I'm saying, "Let's just go see —"

"Hey, what about behind that playground?" Barney said. "That look like a house to you?"

"It's a school," I told him.

So Barney pulled up to the playground parking lot, cut the lights, and got out. "Hey, Barn," I said, "what're you doing? It's a goddamn school. Anybody can see it's a goddamn school." I turned around and said to ol' Silent Sam in the back, "Long Tall, tell him it's a —" But Long Tall wasn't listening. He was watching Barney trudge off into the dark. The two of us just sat there. Damn crickets were going creek-creek-creek-creek, and you couldn't hear any sound other. I mean, no party sounds, just dead-quiet-dead behind the creek-creek-creek. I started feeling bad again. I started wondering why in the hell I was out there with those guys. What possessed me to — Man, God, and Monkey, I was thinking, am I nuts? Out here running around with these two shit birds who're drunk and toting guns. What is it with guys who go to other guys and say, "Help me, man, I gotta get laid"? I'm not talking about a blind date or something. I'm talking sex. Sex, I was saying to myself, that stuff's private. Why is it when a guy — lemme tell you something. Guys are really screwy when it comes to sex. Lemme tell you:

I remember four of us jarheads drove down to Tijuana to buy Christmas junk for our folks. Then after about three hours we were tired as hell and thirsty so we went to this little matchbox with a liquor license. Everybody's downing their booze and I'm knocking down 7-Ups and acting just as drunk as they were. Then these four Mexican chicks came from nowhere and asked to sit with us. Everybody says fine, and I turned to this guy, Corporal Rawlins, nudged him with my elbow, and said, "Can you believe our luck? Four guys, four chicks. Great, huh?" He looked at me with his mouth twisted and his eyes slit. "Man, what're you, a comedian? Ever'-gawdamn-bawdy knows 'ere's a whorehouse right across the street. The bartender just gits on th' horn whenever jarheads come in here and rings up whatever number he needs." I said something like, "Oh yeah, that's right. I always forget."

Anyway, the women, all of 'em pretty, but a little hefty and over made-up, well, they start loving us up, leaning over in their low-cut dresses, rubbing our legs, licking their lips. "Time to go to woik," Grapehead said. And we all stood up together and went across the street to the whorehouse. We went up into this place that looked like the Compton projects and went up these piss-smelling stairs and into this bedroom. All right now, so we all walk into this room and the women run around and start lighting candles. One of 'em plugs in a lava lamp. Another one pops a cassette into this little portable deck, and it's, like, a Pink Floyd tape or something. She started doing this come-hither dance with one of the guys. My "date" pulled at my belt and swayed to the music. I looked her over. She was pretty, about my age at the time. Except she had this enormous beehive and a pink shift that was about sixty ka-billion years out of style. It put me off a bit. I check out the room a second. There're six beds in the room. Six beds, little metal single-framed suckers with no bedding on 'em at all. Just naked mattresses with stains all over 'em. And then it hit me. These women are gonna screw us out in the open! On these beds! With no room dividers, no sheets or blankets to cover up with! Aiiieee! You gotta know that if I couldn't go to the bathroom with a buncha guys standing around looking, you know I ain't gonna get laid — especially for the very first time — where an audience can check out my every stroke. I said, "Hey, Grape, gimme your keys, man. We're going out to the car." Grape was already out of everything but his skivvies, and he wasn't too quick about getting me the keys. I think he was waiting for his hard-on to recede a bit.

So, the woman and I got into the car, and immediately she started to pull up her dress and slip off her panties. I was pretty damned excited. I took her face in my hands and moved to kiss her, but she said, "No kissing, please. Blow job seven dollars, fucking, twenty dollars." That was enough passion for me, dude. I told her to forget it. She started cussing me out till I gave her ten bucks. I told her to split. And I just sat there and waited for the guys to come back. Well, they did come back, and this is what I mean by how weird some dudes can be about sex. All the way back to Camp Pendleton they were saying things like, "Joo hear that bitch moanin? I believe she came twice."

"Haw-haw, what the hell you talkin 'bout, nigro. She was screamin 'cause a your breath."

"Naw, he paid 'er an extra five bucks to scream. Hey, hey, did you see how long that one I had gimme skull?"

"Yeah, an' I saw you give her some, too, man. Haw-haw!"

I mean, God. I mean, Jeez, they watched each other, competed with each other. I don't get it. And the first time I ever heard of a circle jerk was when I was in the service. And some of the more, you know, well-endowed guys actually had hard-on contests. What is it with guys like this? I didn't want to show folks what a man I was. Not that way. What I wanted was something private. Well, I guess I wanted, well . . . OK, love. How can they be so —

Well, Long Tall and I were sitting there, waiting for Barn, who'd been gone for about three, four minutes. The crickets were going creek-creek, and if I'd had any idea where Barney'd gone, I would have gone out to look for him. Instead I sat back in my seat and said, "Long Tall." I said, "Why is this guy so outta control? Why does he do stuff like this? Why can't he just let stuff be?" Long Tall was quiet for a half a minute or so, and I turned around to see if he was asleep. He was awake. It's just that he was trying to roll a joint in that weak light. Very slowly. Carefully, you know? "Where'd you get the pot?" I said. He licked the joint and lit up, offered it to me, but I said no. "My sock," he said. He huffed and blew.

Then the guy said, "I'm getting out pretty soon, Bones. When I'm gone you got to help Barn all you can." He was quiet for a second 'cause he was huffing some more. Then he said, "Barney's crazy, man. Barney's very, very in-sane."

What freaked me the most was that Long Tall didn't say "Heh-heh-heh," or anything like that. The way he said it was like a guy might say, Barney's dead, man. Barney ate his parents, man. Barney serves Satan, man. Look, I knew the guy was crazy, but I thought it was like that guy in *Cuckoo's Nest*, McMurphy. A show, so people wouldn't mess with him. But when Long Tall said, "Barney's crazy, man," it hit me as to just what kind of crazy he was. Pretty soon, I could hear Barney cursing all the way back to the bus. "Gawddmndmu-thafluffinshitratbastard," and like that. He snatched the door open, hopped in, and we were off. He didn't even bother to close the door for a block or two. My boy was all hunched up over the wheel, and his beady black eyes looked like they were focused on the windshield instead of the road. And my boy was actually drooling. If I'm lying may I bake like a ham in hell. I was expecting his nails to start growing, and hair and fangs and all that nonsense. He was still mumbling and muttering under his breath and I caught mostly the usual curse words: *fluffamuffinragnastyfuhcheesitssake*, but when I heard the boy say ". . . something for their asses," I freaked. "You're not going back there, are you?" I said.

Long Tall told me to never mind.

"What the hell you mean, 'never mind,' gotdamnit, he's got a gun and he's pissed off." I wanted to ask Long Tall why, if he was asking me to help the guy, was he telling me to never mind.

But I said, "Barney, damnit, look —"

But Barney told me to shut up. I did, not because he said so, but because I could feel my heart beating in my neck. And you know how tears come to your eyes when you're really pissed off? Like you're not crying or anything, but your eyes are so full of tears you have to wipe them away? I think when a lot of guys get that way, that's when they start swinging or stabbing, shooting or what have you. Watery as my eyes were, I checked out the speedometer and we were doing close to seventy-five. Seventy-five, man! On a residential street. Whoom, voom, ka-floom! In no time we got back to the place where we'd said adios to Eddie. I tried to grab hold of Barney's arm, but he yanked it away and was gone, sprinting full out, that silver gun flashing away in the dark. "Be right back," said Long Tall, and he started out of the bus. But then we heard a woman scream, and we heard Barney whooping, then we heard two shots and glass was all over my lap. Long Tall and I were out of the bus and on the deck so low and tight you'd think we was covered with suction cups. Next thing you know, Barney's back at the bus, yelling "Let's rock." He was grinning like a Vegas show girl. We zapped back in and we were gone. Barney had one hand on the wheel, and with his left he popped off two or three shots. I think Long Tall was blazing away, too, but I couldn't see. I was crammed between the seat and the floorboard. There was more screaming, but in no time it faded. We were moving. We were a time machine.

I knew we weren't going back to Pendleton. Barney wasn't done. I just knew it. What he did was circle around and around the neighborhood just in case those guys'd tried to follow us, then he motored back to Eddie's house. I can't tell you how deep down in my belly my heart'd sunk. Yeah, one second it felt like it was in my throat, and the next it was competing for space with my huevos. Old Long Tall was back to his heh-heh-heh business, and he said, "What'd I tell you, Bones. Ain't done yet." Barney and Long Tall got out and went straight to the garage. I sat there, eyeballing the keys in the ignition, looking behind me so's to check out whether we'd been followed, looking around expecting SWAT teams, helicopters, mace, grenades, looking at them as the two of 'em knelt before the garage. They were obviously picking the lock. The garage door rolled up in just a couple minutes. I couldn't help myself after that. I had to see what Barney was going to do. I hopped out and joined them. "Find the light switch, guys," Barney said, and it took us a while, but Barney found it by the door that led to the house.

Barney uncovered the Harley as I knew he would pretty much from the second I recognized the house. His voice was calm when he said, "Gimme your gun, L.T." Long Tall handed it over. Barney stuffed Long Tall's gun into his pants and then aimed his own gun at the beautiful blue tank. I exchanged looks with Long Tall, and he just threw up his hands. "Bye-bye, girl-friend," Barney said, but just before he squeezed off the first round, the side door squeaked open and Barney swung his gun right at the open door. No one came through for a few seconds and I could see Barney's hand trembling. I could see the dirt under his thumbnail. I could see every single hair on his arm. I could see the veins on his wrist, and I even thought I could see the blood moving through them veins. But the funny thing was, you know, the last thing I noticed was — even though I'd been hanging with these guys a month or two, even though I'd seen Barney naked, seen him sleeping, and eating and drugging. Even though, I'm telling you, my friend, that I'd seen him get his arm stitched up after he'd knocked his fist through a half dozen windows. It took me all this time to see the green, red, and blue tattoo on his arm — a skull with a bloody dagger jammed into it, and under the skull was this fancy-looking scroll that read DEATH BEFORE DIS-HONOR. Jesus Bob Christ, I thought.

Then we heard the whir of an electric motor, and

then we heard that French horn voice. "Eduardo? Eduardo?" And slow as a minute hand, little sister came rolling down the ramp and into the garage. She didn't scream or anything, but you could tell what she was feeling. Real quiet, the French horn said, *"Donde esta mi hermano?"*

Now, I was standing right between Long Tall and Barney, see, and Barney was standing forty-five degrees to me. I could see his eyes. They squinted just enough for me to see what he was thinking, or might have been thinking. Not one of us moved. I don't even think any of us breathed. I could hear crickets, and cars and voices way off in the distance. I could hear the house contracting. I could hear the bones in my own body creaking. I could hear the T.V. in the house. It's funny, all the little stuff you notice when you're scared like that. But as soon as I moved, I could only hear the sound of the blood rushing through my ears. I moved slowly, but nothing was gonna stop me. I walked up to the girl, without looking at Barney or Long Tall. I dropped to my knees, and I put my arms around her. I closed my eyes. I couldn't understand why I'd done that. Actually, I was just gonna stand in front of her, face Barney off like a real hero type. But when I saw how scared she was . . . I don't know, I guess I kind of could see how scared I was. I think I just needed to hug somebody. The weird thing was that she didn't freak out when I did that. I think she knew what I was doing. Maybe more than I did. I didn't say anything. Nobody said anything. Little sister wasn't crying or anything, and I couldn't tell if I was shaking or she was. She wasn't making any sound at all. I held on to her, expecting a bullet to punch out the back of my head any second. I wasn't gonna let go of her, though. I listened to her heart beat and I heard her gulp every now and then. I held her till my knees hurt and my back hurt and till my hands got all sweaty from her heat. Then she said, in perfect English, "They're gone."

So I stood up and pulled my bones and muscles back into place. I took hold of the wheelchair handles and helped her back into the house. I turned out the garage lights, went out the big door, and closed it. I was surprised to see my two friends sitting in the bus, smoking cigarettes, waiting for me. I climbed in, Barney cranked her up, and we split back to Pendleton. Even though we never discussed it you just knew we weren't gonna visit July and Carly. We were quiet the whole way. When we got to the parking lot, Barney turned half right to me and just looked at me. He stared at me for an awful long time, as though he was expecting me to say something. But I'm telling you right here and now, dude, I hadn't a thing to say. I just wanted to get out of that bus and put as much distance between me and those guys as I could, but Barney's stare held me right there in my seat. And Barney kept staring, and I kept staring back, but just before I was fixing to say, Barney, L.T., you guys are some sick pups, or something like that, finally Barney said, "Well, Bones, was it good for you?" And then he leaned toward me quick as a cobra and kissed me right smack-dab dead on the lips like he was some kinda damn Warner Brothers cartoon character. Barney and Long Tall cracked up, laughing and backslapping like a couple of idiots. I sat and spat and spat and spat. But I got to admit I was kinda laughing too. What the hell else could I do?

Hey, tell me something, what is it with guys, anyway?

Into Night

/ / / / / /

At two-thirty in the afternoon last Tuesday, just like every day, Sandman got to be as restless as a ghost. Didn't he nor I nor his mama know why he got this way. It mighta had something to do with two-thirty being the time that *Cartoon Tyme* went off the air. That meant to Sandman they wasn't nothing on the box till six in the evening, when *Gimme a Break* come on. Sandman liked that show a whole bunch 'cause it have this big ol' fat woman on it who look like my daughter Erlene and who holler like everybody she talking to a mile away. From two-thirty on, wasn't nothing on but news, game shows, and soaps, programs a five-year-old cain't stand. But I know that didn't have all that much to do with why my grandchild got as fidgety as he did most every day. Most likely it had to do with the fact that his big sister, Tanika, was fend to arrive home from school before long. And little Tanika had what I call a unnatural ability for knowing if Sandman done been in

117

her room, messing with her things, which he did most every day.

Don't know what it was about that boy. Seem like he just couldn't break hisself away from going up to her room. Been doing that since Pauline, my daughter, and her husband, Ricardo, moved me in with them last winter. Didn't know what it was. The child has plenty of his own toys and things. He like to drive his mama and his sister and his daddy insane every day with his constant going up to her room and messing with her things. Even though things have changed since Tuesday last, I still think they should put the boy in preschool, like they done Tanika, but they won't. Pauline say, "Mama, they ain't nothing they can teach him at that school that I cain't teach him at home." Course she say it a whole lot prettier and fancier than that, 'cause of all the education she's had, but that's basically what she said. I know she get irritated with me sometimes, and I hates to interfere and get in the way, but I see what I see, and I know what I know. The boy don't mean no harm. When they first brung me here last winter, after Paul passed, I thought they wanted me to help with the chi'ren, and this big ol' house, but it seem like granmas is better seen and not heard. Seem like all they want me to do is sit around the house and crochet and look thankful I got family. Lord, I coulda did that back in Shreveport. Didn't need to come up here.

Now, the "crime of crimes," as far as Tanika was concerned, was "even breathing" on her model aero-planes. Ricardo fond of saying that Tanika is "uncanny" at remembering exactly where she set each and every model she had displayed round her room. But Sandman loves the models as much as his sister do, and he show his love for 'em by playing with 'em. But sometimes he break 'em, too. After a while, though, he got used to Tanika's temper, I suppose, even though the girl can explode like a bone-dry radiator when she want to, and even though she take forever to cool back down. He got used to, too, with her always screaming 'bout how her models is not toys and how "ab-so-loot-ly nooo-body" under nine years old is allowed in her room. That girl can screech and squeak, shake that one itty-bitty fist in his face, threaten the boy with "fis' soup and knuckle samwiches" till she near 'bout blue in the face. But Sandman steady been in her room and steady play with her models. And ol' Sandman'll stand up in fronta Tanika like a deacon stand up before the altar to receive holy reprimand. He stand tall as he can in front of her and try not to look too bored or too sassy. The boy'll stay cool as ice cream, little as he is, nodding every now and then, but not saying a word. Now, before Tuesday, however, when Tanika'd be in a 'specially nasty mood she'd smack Sandman upside his head. And just like any sinner ought to fear one of the Lord's crackly lightning bolts, Sandman was afred of his sister's hurricane swings and lightning knuckles. But things been pretty calm since Tuesday last, like I said.

Well, the light from the T.V. shrunk down to a tiny

dot and faded away. I was sitting up in the living room with him, at the time, and I looked up from my crocheting and watched him watch hisself get up from his Cap'n Starheart Official Star Command T.V. cushion, and glide on out the living room. Looked to me, at first, he was going down to the basement where his mama's studio at, but I said, "Uh-uh, baby, Mama's busy. Whyn't you stay up here with Granmama. You hungry?" He said he wasn't hungry.

"Well," I said, "I think you ought to go out'n play in the back, or you can take a nap, then."

He didn't say nothing for about a minute, just stood there, standing on the side of his shoes like he always do, so I said, "Baby, don't stand that way, you'll ruin your shoes. You wanna go out?" But he said he didn't wanna go out, said he wanted to take a nap. Well, I knew something was up. Ain't seen many five-year-old boys ask for a nap, but I said, "All right. You want me to go up with you and pat your back?" and he shook his head no, and went on up the stairs. I knew what he was gonna do. He was gonna go right straight up them stairs and go right on into Tanika's room. Don't know who he thought he was fooling. This an old house, and when it's quiet here, you can hear every creak and croak them steps and them floorboards make. Once somebody up on the landing, ain't but a half dozen or so sounds you gonna hear: If it's Sandman's room you gonna hear, "Grunt-grunt" — that's to the right. If it's Tanika's room it's gon' be, "Grunt-grunt-o-gruncha?"

The bathroom say, "Grunt-grunt-o-pop," or "Grunt-grunt-o-squeak-pop," depending on whether you step on the doorsill or not. The rooms on the left, mine's and the master bedroom, have their own way, too. Didn't even have to get out my chair to know Sandman went up them twelve steps, and instead of going to his room: "Grunt-grunt," I heard, "Grunt" . . . and a long pause, and then . . ."grunt," and then a long, long, long pause, and then — he was sneaking, see — "o-gruncha?" I just had to laugh. And then right when I was thinking 'bout going up after him, Pauline hollered from downstairs, "Mama? Where Sandman at?" See, only a mama could have that kind of feeling that her child ain't up to no good. "Oh, he upstairs," I yelled back. "Napping."

She was quiet for a little bit, then she said, "Would you check on him for me, please?"

"All right, honey," I said. And I tiptoed up them dozen steps, thinking I'd peep at him in his sister's room for a bit before picking his narrow behind up and putting him in his own room. He just love Tanika's room and Tanika's things, but I myself can't stand it. Don't like the smell. Smells like model glue, strawberry talcum powder, and doll plastic. Child must have a thousand dolls in that room, and every one of 'em different. Different colors, different doll tricks, different sizes and shapes. But I'll tell you one thing: ain't never seen the girl play with a one. Most every one a them dolls was sent to her by her and Sandman's granmama who live in Tennessee. That woman just cain't stand the idea a my grandbaby being interested in model planes. Ricardo's mother got a little . . . money, see, and she like everybody to know it, so every chance she get she send Tanika some kinda doll. Don't matter what occasion it is, Christmas, Easter, Tanika's birthday, Sandman's birthday, good report card, bad report card, no report card, or "just for being a sweet thing," don't make no never mind. Woman like to make me spit up. The child got an army a dolls, a legion a dolls that cry, belch, sing, snore, pee, drink, get diaper rash, walk, blink, crawl. But Tanika, bless her heart, won't touch 'em.

If you's to walk into her room on any day, you wouldn't see a one of these dolls. But you can smell 'em. They crammed into her closet, stacked under her bed. Ain't but two or three of 'em ever even been removed from they boxes. Ricardo call Tanika's bedroom "the bone yard," and even joked about buying a plastic wreath to hang on her door. But Pauline didn't find that funny at all. Said Ricardo's sense of humor is morbid. Her and her fancy words — but I agree with her. Talk like that will only give the babies bad dreams.

Well, I opened up Tanika's door just a tee-nine-chee bit and peeked in, and Lord, what did I see. Lord, it made me put my hand to my chest, and made my eyes bug out, and made my breathing like to stop. I seen Sandman standing in the middle of Tanika's room spinning round slow like somebody dancing by hisself, and flying round and round was one of Tanika's aero-planes going round and round the room. I didn't mean to speak so loud, but I hollered, "Sandman!" and the boy jecked his head my way and the plane went zing and smacked right into the door. I jumped back. Well, before I could collect myself and open the door, I heard Pauline's footsteps on the stairs and she saying in her shrieky-high voice, "What's going on up there? What's that boy doing?" I opened up the door just as Pauline got up the stairs. "Paul," I was fend to say, but Pauline said, "Maxwell Sanders Harris! Boy, what'd I tell you about playing in your sister's room?" Pauline very light skinned like her daddy, and when she get upset like she was then, she get this maroon blush on her face, look just like a butterfly. Her daddy, Paul, used to color up the very same way, and so do Tanika. I'll tell you what, when they get to wearing that maroon butterfly, you better look out. "Huh, boy?" Pauline said. "What'd I say?"

"Not to," Sandman said.

"Then why'd you do it, huh?"

Sandman didn't say nothing, and I felt just turrible for the child. He stood there, as he always do on the side of his feet, with his hands behind his back, and his forehead creased, his eyes looking all worried. Like to make me cry. Had on his little suspenders, his little blue jeans a size or two too big. Big head, little scrawny neck. I just felt turrible, looking at that boy, and I said, "Paul, now you got work to do, honey. Let me talk to him."

"Mama, I been talking to this child enough to make my head spin. I'm damn sick and tired of him defying me. Damn sick and tired of it."

"Ain't no reason to cuss me, girl," I said. "I'm your —"

"Mind your bidness — boy, get to your room."

Sandman is usually a well-behaved child, but for some reason he didn't budge. Instead, he looked at my feet and he said, "Mama, that plane flew by itself." Then quick as you could blink, *whap!* Pauline slapped his face. "Oww!" he said, real slow and long. He opened his mouth wide and his eyes got big, and tears filled up his eyes. He put his hand on his face where Pauline'd hit and tears was just rolling, but he didn't make no crying sounds at all. Then again he said, "Oww."

"What'd I tell you about lying?" Pauline said.

"Pauline!" I said.

"Get to your room, boy!"

Whap! She hit him again.

"Pauline!"

And Sandman hunched over and he looked like he couldn't believe what his mama was doing. He opened his mouth wide and saliva was dripping in a long string from his mouth and there was that silent crying for a long, long time. You know how chi'ren be when they gots to rear up they breath before they starts to really let loose. That's just what Sandman did. And Lord-a-mighty he did let loose. Loud. Then he walked past us and went to his room, still all hunched over, still with his hand on his face, just wailing and wailing and wailing. "Shut up that crying," Pauline said. Then she turned to me and the butterfly was like to fly off her face, it was so hot and red. "What you got to say, Mama. Huh? What you got to say?"

And I looked at the boy walk into his room, then I looked at the aero-plane on the floor of Tanika's room, and I seen the fishing line tied to it, and I understood why it looked like the plane'd been flying. See, some of Tanika's models is on chrome stands, and some of 'em hangs from fishing lines from the ceiling. Ricardo give her the line, you understand. Apparently, what happened was the boy'd found something long to smack the plane with and make it fly in a circle like it did. But it was going so fast, I told myself, I couldn't see the line at first. But there it was, just as plain as day, tied onto the aero-plane, and at the other end of the line was the thumbtack that had held the line in the ceiling. I felt foolish, 'cause I was fend to tell Pauline that the plane did too fly. Seen it with my very own eyes, I was gonna say. But looked like I was wrong, so I didn't know what to say about that. The sound a Sandman's crying made me hurt in my chest and in my throat. Don't know why it upset me so. Ain't like I've never heard chi'ren cry before. And I really didn't wanna interfere with how my grown daughter raise her chi'ren. I might be her mama, but I'm a guest in this house. I got to respects what they say and do. Pauline is a good and strong woman, and I'm so proud of what she's done and what she's got. The child's got statues standing, and pictures hanging, in museums in Detroit and California and New York City, and here in Pittsburgh. Sometimes she take me down into her studio in the basement and show me what she working on. The stuff she do is so pretty, all them loud African colors, like a store full of jaw-breakers. Like to make your mouth water. I got to admit I don't care for everything she do, and I think she ought to put some more clothes on some of those women she paint and draw, and not make their faces look so cross, but I guess she know what she doing, and I guess I don't. But the one she working on now, the one she shown me a day or two ago, she call *The Vanishing Blue*, which she tell me is about that Middle Passing, I believe it is, when the white folks took our people from Africa. Well, it's all done in blue dots, like a million tiny blue dots, this one picture, see. Blues so light they nearly white, to blues so dark, they nearly black. And its animals and birds and trees, and it all look like you seeing down from way, way up in the air. Like you done passed from this life, and you looking down on every-thing. That one I like, and I understand it. But even if I don't understand or don't like something, I don't say anything. No, sir, I don't. She grown, and it's her life. Besides, she got them two fine chi'ren and a good hus-band who she tell me is the best optometrist in town. They got a nice house. They got two nice cars. And they been so good to me.

But I had to say something. I mean, she was standing there in front of me, huffing and puffing with her hands on her hips, and her butterfly a-burning. She looked so tired, had beeswax under her fingernails, and what looked like charcoal on her cheek, a rope a that dreadful Rooster, Rasta, Roster hair, or whatever you calls it, hanging down over one eye. One wrong word might make things worse, I was thinking, and like I say, I didn't want to interfere, but when you looks at it the way a five-year-old do, that plane was flying. So I said, "It's my fault, baby. I was supposed to be watching him, and I wasn't. Don't be too hard on him."

"Mama," she said, and then she pointed her finger at me, which she know I don't like, "I have told him and told him and told him —"

"I know —"

"— to stay out of his sister's room. And I'm sick of it. And you know good and well you raised me to despise lying. Now, you got anything else to say?"

"No."

"Good." And she spun around and went. Sounded like a herd a buffalo going down them steps. Then I heard her holler up the stairs, "And, Mama, please leave that mess he made right where it is, till Ricardo and Tani get home. And Maxwell, boy, don't you let me hear you fooling around up there. You get your butt into that bed and stay quiet."

Well I did leave the "mess" where it was. I didn't feel like doing anything no how. Sandman was still in his room, gasping and whooping like his room didn't have no air in it. I shut his door, then went on into my own room and closed my door, too. I could still hear him a little bit. I wanted to go into his room and hold him a spell, but that was for his mama to do. If she'd come back upstairs for some reason, and seen me doing that, why, I think she'd a got upset all over again. Didn't know what to do with myself, so I just kicked off my shoes, pulled off my glasses, untucked my blouse, un-fastened the top button of my pants, and laid down on my bed.

Just before my eyes got heavy, I heard a sound that said, "Doomp, d-doom doomp. Doomp, d-doom doomp," kinda like the way that Sergeant Joe Friday music go. I knew it was Sandman fiddling around with something, and I got up and out my room in my stock-ing feet, stood outside the door to his room, and lis-tened. He was talking to hisself, real quiet like. And the sound said, "Doomp, d-doom doomp." Got down on my knees and looked through the keyhole. Sandman was sitting on his toy box, his chin resting in his hands, bouncing his heels off the side of the toy box. "Doomp, d-doom doomp." Then he hopped down off the box, th'ew it open, and started digging through it. After a good deal of digging and searching and looking, he took out this little rubber super-hero doll — didn't know what its name was, only ones I know is Superman, Batman, and that Starheart fella he so crazy about, but this one I didn't know; besides, I couldn't see it all that well no how, since I didn't have my glasses on.

Well now, he closed the lid on the box, and stood the doll up on its feets, and backed up a few steps from the box. I could just barely see the doll's head poking up over Sandman's shoulder. What is he doing? I asked myself. Then he pointed his finger at the doll, and said in the loudest whisper he could, "Fly, Spiderman!" Well, I be dogged, I was thinking. Maybe he can too, make things fly. "Fly, Spiderman!" he said again. Almost made me laugh out loud. Then the boy said, "Shazzam!" and then when that didn't work, he said, "Eeeeagle Power!" then, "By the Power of Greeey-skuuull," "Up, up, and awaaaay," and "Spaaaace Ghooost!" and his voice kept getting louder and louder, till I knew I better go on in there and tell him to hesh up before his mama come up and peel his behind. I stood up, and Lord did my knees argue with me. Used to be only on cloudy days when my arthur-itis trouble me, but since I come up here, it seem like just about a daily thing.

Well, I took ahold of the doorknob, and just as I twisted it, I heard Sandman holler, "Tired-ass punk," and I heard him th'ow the doll against the wall. It tickled me; I just had to laugh. But soon's I opened the door, I heard Pauline running back up the stairs. Reckon she wasn't in her studio at all, but in the kitchen, and since Sandman's room is right smack over the kitchen, she musta heard every sound he was making.

Well, she pushed right on past me without so much as a how do, and slammed the door shut, and I heard *whap! whap!* and it started up all over again. Lord-a-mighty it was a ugly sound. I just couldn't bear to hear it. I couldn't stand there two seconds. I went to my room and closed the door, laid on my bed, pressed the heels of my hands over my ears, but I could hear every sound. I heard the boy crying, and I heard Pauline barking just like a dog. "You little bastard, what'd I tell you? Huh? Huh?" Heard the sound of hangers sliding back and forth on the rod in Sandman's closet. Knew she was looking for a belt. She found one, too, 'cause I heard every one of them strokes. Every single one. And every now and then I heard that boy say things like, "Mama? Mama? I love you. I love you," and I heard hard things hitting the floor and I knew they was heels or elbows or knees or noggin. I knew the boy was burning up, scared, in a devil wind of hurt. I knew Pauline was hurting, too, blind, sick, dizzy, excited, and hurting her ownself. But I knew, also, that she didn't know it. I heard, "What I say?" and "black bastard" and "skin you alive" and "don't you dare raise your hand to me." I heard "please" and "sorry" and "didn't mean to" and "forgot to" and "love you, Mama, love you." But I knew Mama couldn't hear a thing but that hissing sound you hear, and blood and heat and ice and nightmares and howling, and the fire on her very own skin — heard it, *heard* it, not seen it — heard the flame tips of memory, and right behind it I heard the hurt of every single one a my babies, Erlene and Justine, Peter, Paul, Mark, and Juline, Pearline and John,

Samuel and Pauline. Pauline. I heard my hands on Pauline, my leather on Pauline, switch, cord, ruler, hanger, towel, wet and heavy. And I heard me, too, my own screams, and my brothers and sisters, my mama, papa, aunts, and uncles and on back, and on back. All that sickening hissing fire. Heard it quivering in my belly, and balling up in my throat . . . and on back and on back. I put my pillow over my head and heard my tears soak into it. Generations and generations of slaves and slavekeepers I heard. I couldn't escape that sound, and I couldn't understand why it was only now I was hearing just how turrible it is. I heard burning crosses and natureless men, women split open like pigs' knuckles, heard the pain of vanishing blue jungles and dry red soil, black long-tooth cats that creep in the night, white long-neck birds that could fill up a blue blue sky. All vanishing into endless ocean and ships full of stink and death. I heard the weight of a thousand leagues of water on my back, heard the howl of a million lost spirits black and white, and black and red, and black and blue. Then just black, so black I couldn't hear nothing no more, nor see, nor breathe, nor move. I wisht I coulda helped that boy, but I couldn't move.

Well, let me see can I go on. Let me get my mind right.

Naturally, Tanika had a hissy fit. Her voice poked me outta my sleep like Paul's skinny elbow used to. Didn't leave my room just then, but I knew her caramelly skin was lit up with the butterfly, them wingtips touching her temple to temple. "But Daddy," I heard her say, "that was my favorite plane."

They were in her bedroom. I could tell.

"Seem like to me," said her father, "that whichever model your brother break is your favorite." He talk kinda pretty, too, when he ain't too upset, so I cain't say it exactly the way he did. "You ever notice that?" he said.

"Well, I guess . . . I like 'em all the same. They all my favorites. That's why I builds 'em."

Then Ricardo said back, "Uh-huh." Then his voice changed a notch. "Maybe we *ought* to put a lock on her door till ol' Sandman old enough to do like he ast."

"But Daddy, he is old enough. He five. He be in school next year."

"No," said Pauline. "I will not abide locks on these chi'ren's doors. Naw-aw. No."

"Awright, Pauline, calm down." And Ricardo's voice changed back. "I know he five, babygirl, but that's still young. You just got to learn patience. Let's just be patient for now. Now, it might make you happy if I tear his little seater-end up —"

"Yes it would!"

"Don't you backtalk your father, girl."

"— but since your mother already done that, I don't see no reason to. We all done seen enough of that around this house."

"You the one to talk, man."

"Hey, I didn't say I'm some kinda saint. I said 'we.' 'We.' "

They was all of 'em quiet for a spell. Then Ricardo
said, "Patience, babygirl. You got to learn patience.
And it's only one way to learn patience." And then he
was quiet for a real long time. "How?" said Tanika.
Then I heard Ricardo carry his big self down the stairs.
He was chuckling. "How?" Tanika said, and Ricardo
laughed a little harder. "How?" Tanika said. "Daddy,
how?" Ricardo just laughed, and I heard Tanika following him, and it sound like she smacked him on the
behind. "Dad-dy!" she said. I had to smile.

I heard Pauline close Tanika's door and open up
Sandman's. Heard her switch on the light and close the
door. The only thing I could hear her say was, "You
hungry, baby?" and I knew she'd be sitting him on her
lap, and wrapping her arms around him. Knew she be
rocking him and cooing to him. And her voice be like a
warm wind full of spices. She might look him over
careful, thinking 'bout, "Maybe I ought to put some
Mercurochrome right there, and a little bit back here,
too, maybe." She cain't believe what she done, you see.
Cain't even remember all of it, really. I knew Sandman
be trembling inside, just like a day-old puppy tremble
when it find itself too far from its mama's belly and
teats. Then it be like he feel the sun rising in his stomach, and maybe he cry a little bit, and say he sorry, and
Mama will feel her heart ease into twos and fours and
eights, breaking real slow and silent, and she'll cry
some too. Try to make him smile, she will, by saying
things like, "You knows you a little hellion, boy. But
you know Mama love her little rascal." And when she

see him smile, her heart'll ease itself from eights to fours to twos and she'll thank Jesus that cain't nobody forgive and forget like a child. She'll get down on her knees and thank Jesus.

But I was sitting there asking myself, What if, after all that holding, after they done eaten and talked and everybody in bed, and Sandman laying there in the dark, what things'll be going through his head when it look like everything back to normal? For my daughter may believe that chi'ren forget, but I know better now. What'll he be thinking? Did I make that plane fly? Was it magic? Is Tanika a witch? Is that why I ain't never allowed to touch them planes? Maybe the whole family is witches — Tanika, Mama, Daddy, Granmama. Maybe late at night they all shrink down to the size of crickets, get inside them planes, and fly to China and New York and Disneyland. Why don't they take me? Maybe they hate me. Maybe they kill if I keep messing with them planes. 'Cause Mama say, "I'ma kill you, boy. I swear I'ma kill you, you don't do as I say." Did I make it fly? Or was it Daddy's fishing line made it fly?

Well, I guess that plane musta flew, all right, 'cause that night, last Tuesday night, we all seen something I don't think we'll ever forget. This is what happened:

I passed on dinner that evening. Just couldn't see sitting down with 'em and getting in their way. Wanted 'em to be just they own family that night. I went to bed, but I couldn't sleep. I tossed and turned in that bed, and it squeaked and squawked, and just about drove me outta my mind. It was a warm night and clear for a night in Pittsburgh, and I went to the window, got down on my knees to pray. I felt like I had to pray against all them sounds I'd heard in my sleep that afternoon, all that pain that been burned into my skin and found its way out my very own hands. Generations and generations. But I couldn't find no words. I looked out that window, and I watched that empty night sky. Never had noticed how big the sky is before, even though I'm in my seventy-seventh year, and seen maybe ten, twenty, thirty thousand such skies. Never noticed how deep it was neither. The very idea of a endless sky made me dizzy, I tell you the truth. I cletched on to the windowsill like I was afred I might fall up and up and up, and keep on falling. I set there a long time on my knees like that, till my arthur-itis started fussing, till the sky turned from dark blue like one of Sandman's cleary marbles to black as a skillet. The clouds was almost invisible. Sky got deeper. Stars began to bleed out from the darkness. It was a glory to behold. "Thank you, Lord," I said. "Thank you." I don't know why I said that.

Next thing I heard was Tanika's elbow voice, poking me outta my sleep once more. "What you doing in my room, boy?" I heard her say. I pulled myself off the cool floor, and my knees and ankles couldn't slow me down none. Not really. Mothers is like that when they hear a child's voice in the night. Don't nothing slow 'em, not arthur-itis, or flu, or migraine, or dropsy. I heard heels and toes hit the floor, robes being pulled on, lights snapped on, doors open. Then Tanika said, "What? You want what?" And just as I was stepping into her room Sandman said, "Granmama, Tani won't teach me to fly her planes." He had a plane in his hand, and it looked like Tanika didn't know it till I did, 'cause her sleepish eyes got big and she screamed, "My Thunderbolt!" Just then Pauline stepped up behind me and her voice cut acrost the room. She said, "What the hell is going on here?" and just about this time Tanika was duking up a storm. Her lips was pushed up into her mouth, nostrils flaring. She chopped at Sandman, and chopped again, had the blind look in her eyes, and knew she heard the hiss. I could hear it. I could hear in that child's head like they was vipers from down below. Pauline was fend to push me out the way, but all in a second I'd grabbed her by her sleeve and hollered, "Tanika, put your hand down, girl! Put it down right this second!"

"Mama, just —"

But I said, "No." I heard that turrible, turrible hissing I know so well and I thought it was me who was gonna start chopping with my hands or with a belt or a shoe or anything else in reach, but it didn't feel like it should have. Didn't burn and build up, like it should have, yet I knew I heard that hissing. I know I did. Then we all turned back to the landing when we heard Ricardo say, "Lookit Sandman!" And when we looked from Ricardo to his son we seen that aero-plane in his hand, and the propeller on that thing was spinning like I don't know what, was just hissing, louder and louder, till you couldn't no longer call it a hiss no more, but a buzz. And wasn't too long before we seen that every aero-plane in that room was buzzing. And the spirit was in me, and I moved across the room on the balls of my feet, like I was Tanika's age. "It's a blessing, chi'ren," I said. "We being blessed." The planes on they chrome stands was buzzing. The planes on the ceiling was buzzing, going round and round on them fishing lines. I went to the window and seen the sky was back to being dark blue again. Didn't have no idea I was asleep that long. Anyway, I opened up the window, pulled up the screen, and put my hand out to Sandman. "Go ahead, Sandman. Go on ahead. It's a blessing. We being blessed." So my grandson walked up to me, and I rested my hand on his head, moved him closer to the window. "Go on, baby," I said. "It's a blessing." Then I turned back to look at the others. Ricardo had his hands in his robe pockets and was looking half crossy-eyed with sleep, half joyful in the presence of the Power, like he didn't know up from down. But Tanika and Pauline, well, they looked like twins to each other, all small and grayish. They eyes was big, but they didn't seem to be looking at anything in particlar, and didn't look cross or scared or nothing, and they didn't have no but- terflies on 'em neither. Just stood there, the tall twin behind the short one, a big right hand hooking fingers betwixt the fingers of a little right hand. I looked back down at my grandson, and I said, "Go on, baby."

Well Sandman just opened his hand and let that plane go and it floated off just like I knew it would, and I closed my eyes and listened to them tiny engines. I felt everybody move on up behind me. I felt Pauline's arm slip round my shoulder. Lord, Lord, all them little planes just fanning up tiny breezes all around us. A body'd have to carry a *pe*can for a heart not to be moved by all that. I do believe he would. So me and Sandman, Tanika and Ricardo, and my baby Pauline, well, one by one, we let them things fly into the night. They looked like little dots, little ink dots, in that blue sky. And they sounded like a million honeybees.

They sounded just like a million honeybees.

Quitting Smoking

/ / / / / /

Jan. 16, 1978   Manitou Spgs., CO

Dear B——,

Happy New Year and all that. Man, are you ever hard
to get ahold of. I wrote your ex–ol' lady first, and she
said, and I quote, "As to his whereabouts, well, your
guess is as good as mine. The last I heard he was still
with TWA, but based in London. I do know that he
was suspended for six weeks for giving free tickets to
London to that girlfriend of his. I'm surprised they
didn't flat out fire him." She mainly ranted about how
you only write and send money on your boy's birthday.
She's still pretty pissed off at you, my man. Anyway,
she said that your folks might know and she gave me
their new address and phone # in Texas. I didn't even
know they moved. Anyway, money's been a little tight
lately, and I don't even have a phone at the moment, so I
wrote a card. Didn't here anything for a long time, but

then your kid sister, Mayra, wrote me, and this is what she said: "We got your letter a long time ago, but we don't know excatly where B____ is My brother has moved alot in the last couple of years because of his job. The reason I'm writing you instead of my mother is because my mother is discusted with B____. But she won't tel anybody why. And she says she doesn't know his adress. I know she does but I can't find it any where. But I will look for it and if I find it I will send it to you. My big sister Letonya said if she gets the adress she will send the letter to B____ but I don't think so because she is getting married and is always forgetting to do things. Mamma is discusted with Letonya because she says shes too young to get married. Right now your letter is on the fridge with a magnit on it."

I thought you'd like that, B____.

Then I called TWA. They were kind of nasty, and no help at all. They did tell me you were on leave, though, but wouldn't say where. So, how did I get your address? Letonya came through. She said you were living it up in Madrid for six months, and then you'd be going back to London. I guess she'd be married by now.

I guess you're probably surprised to hear from me after all these years, homes, and I bet you're surprised at how long this letter is, or for me right at this second, how long it's gonna be. This'll be the longest thing I'll ever have written by the time I'm done. I know that already, B____, 'cause the stuff I got on my mind is complicated and confusing. I've been sleeping pretty bad lately, 'cause I've been thinking about that thing that happened when you, me, Stick, and Camel saw that guy snatch that woman into his car in front of Griff's, just after hoops practice. I'm sure you remember. It bothered me a lot back then, of course, but you know it's been nine years now and you get over things like that after a while. And for a long time I didn't really think about it all that much. But something happened a few weeks ago between me and my girlfriend, Anna, that brought all that stuff up again and has pretty much messed up things between me and her. The stuff I'm gonna tell you, speaking of "between," is just between you and me. Period. OK? But I've gotta tell you the whole thing so you'll understand where I'm coming from and understand why I've done what I've done. I feel bad that I've gotta talk about Anna behind her back like this, but goddamnit, you're the only guy who'd understand what I'm trying to work out in my mind. You and me are pretty much cut from the same tree, you could say. We both grew up in this town. Well, I'm in Manitou now and not Colo. Spgs., but I'll get to that later. We both hung around maybe too many white people growing up. We're both tall and black, but can't play hoops worth a damn. We both have had very weird relationships with redheaded, green-eyed women, only you actually married yours. Anna and I just lived together. Yeah, "live" in the past tense. Looks like it might be over between me and Anna. Over, unless, after you've read all this, you think what I've done is wrong, and you say that I should give Anna another chance, or she should give me one. You know, I was gonna try to get in touch with the other "fellas" about this, too. I know where the Stick is. I think I do, anyway. I ran into Coach Ortiz at José Muldoon's and he told me the Stick is teaching poli sci at some college in Athens, Georgia. I'd tried his folks' place first, but the old phone # don't work and they're not in the book. The last I heard about Camel is that he joined the service. The army or the air force, I'm not sure. Can you imagine that big buck-tooth hippie in the service? But anyway, I decided not to write or call those guys 'cause, to be honest, they're white and I don't think they'd understand.

Right now, I'm living in Manitou Springs, like I said, in a place called Banana Manor. A big stone monster painted bright yellow and trimmed in brown. It used to be a hotel, I guess. It's kind of a hippie flophouse. Lots of drugs, sex, rock 'n' roll, long hair, and cheap rent. I got a room here and pay only $65 a month for it. Most of my stuff 's still at the place me and Anna shared, and I still go by there and pick up my mail and stuff, but I only go there when she's not around, mainly 'cause it'd hurt too much to see her. I leave her notes and still pay my share of the rent. Don't know how long I'll do that though.

Before I get to my point (sorry it's taking me so long) I guess I oughta catch you up on me. After all, B——, we ain't seen each other in about six years, or written or called since you split with Kari. How's your boy, by the way? Good, I hope. Well now, I finally got my certificate in cabinetry at Pikes Peak Comm. Col. Actually, I copped an A.A. in general studies, too. I had the money and the time, so I figured, what the fuck. Besides, Anna kept ragging on me till I did. Graduated third in my cabinetry class, quit this stockBOY gig I'd had at Alco's and got a part-timer at Chess King. I sold shake yo' booty clothes to mostly army clowns from Fort Cartoon. (That's what my Anna calls Fort Carson.) Well, I got fired for "studying at work" and "ignoring customers," which all I have to say about is if you remember my study habits in high school, you'll know it was all bullshit. They fired me 'cause I wouldn't wear their silly-ass clothes on the job. My mom always used to tell me, "You ain't got to dress like a nigro to look like a nigro, boy."

So I was out of work for about two months and moved in with Anna, which had its ups and downs (no pun). Anna's got a couple of years on me. Actually five, but she looks about 20. She has a kid, though, and to tell you the truth, I could do without the instant family stuff. But Max, her kid is all right for a rug rat. I mean, he wets the bed sometimes, and he's about as interested in sports as I'm interested in *Sesame Street*, but he's smart, funny, and likes me, so I could hang with it. To tell you the truth, I miss him a lot.

But like I'm saying, there were some good things about living with Anna, and some things that weren't so good. Good and not so good. The usual. She's divorced, and 31, like I said. We met at the community college about a year and a half ago. It was in the Spring Quarter, and the weather was perfect, in the 80's, sky like a blank blue page. I was sitting on a bench outside the cafeteria, talking to this friend of mine, when she walked by in a pink Danskin top and a pink and white flowered skirt. My asshole friend yells out, "Hey! You got the most beautiful breasts I've ever seen." And she blushed and kept walking. I told Steve that was no way to talk to a woman and he told me that broads like that kind of talk, and besides, he didn't say "tits." I told him to screw off and ran after her. I apologized to her and told her I had nothing to do with what Steve'd said. She kind of nodded real quick, mumbled something, and kept walking. Then I walked away, and didn't figure I'd ever see her again. I felt like an idiot. Didn't even wanna think about it.

Well, about two weeks later I was in the parking lot and just about to my car when I hear this little voice say, "You have the most beautiful ass I've ever seen." It was Anna, and as they say, da rest is history. She's 5'2" and has a body that would make your teeth sweat. Steve was right about her bust, but he missed the rest. Like I say, she's got red hair, green eyes, but the weird thing is she tans real good. Not like most redheads who sit out in the sun for two seconds and end up looking like blisters with feet, or get so many freckles that you wanna hand 'em a brown Magic Marker and tell 'em to go finish the job. So anyway, she's also about a hundred times smarter than I am, which is no big deal, 'cause she never jams it down my throat. Besides, since I started at the cabinet mill I make more scratch than she does. (She's on welfare.) Anna's a sociology major at Colorado College now, and she'd been trying to talk me into going there to get a degree in something, but for one thing I don't have the money, and for another thing, you don't exactly see legions of folks our color over there so I doubt they'd want me. Anyhow, I'm not exactly a genius. I might have done good in cabinet school, but I couldn't pull higher than six or seven B's in general studies. Screw 'em. Plus, I know the kind of bullshit you had to put up with at Graceland College, amongst all that wheat and corn and cow squat. I still have that letter where you told me about the "joke" (ha-ha) Klan party your friends threw for you on your birthday. That kind of thing ain't for the kid here.

Anyway, let me get to my point before I bore you to death. OK, so like one night, about a month ago, Anna and I were in the sack and she wouldn't even kiss me good night. This is strange, I was thinking, 'cause usually she's more interested in sex than I am, which means she likes it more than a woodpecker likes balsa. So I asked her what the hell was wrong. (Actually, I said, "Hey, babes, you OK?") And she started crying, real slow and silent. So I got up and burned a doobie. (Yes. I smoke now. Actually, I smoke cigarettes, too, but I'd pretty much quit while I was with Anna. More about that later.) I passed it to her and she took a couple hits. So like I asked her again what was up and she said she got upset 'cause that day in class they were talking about social deviants (sp?) and her prof said that all of society makes it easy for men to commit rape and that there was no real way to completely eradicate it. So Anna said back to the guy that castration would sure the hell stop it. And then nobody said much of anything for like a minute. Then the prof came back with all that talk show crap that rape isn't sexual, but violent, etc., etc. And Anna just sat there for a while, while the guy kept talking, and she told me that she'd made up her mind not to say anything else. But then, before she knew what hit her, she just sort of blared out, "Then give them the fucking death penalty!" That's exactly what she said. And that started a huge argument in the class.

Well, Anna crushed out the joint in the ashtray. She did it real hard and all I could think about was somebody crushing out a smoking hard-on, which I'm sure she wanted me to think. She's really into symbols and shit. In fact, I think she wanted me to get my A.A. just so I'd get all the symbols she dumps on me. All right, so I was kind of surprised, 'cause even though Anna's kind of a women's libber, she's always been pretty mellow about things, and she's always been real anti–death penalty. So I asked her why she'd said that stuff in class. She didn't say anything for about a minute. She was just staring up at the passion plant that we have hanging over our bed. So I asked her if she was ever raped. I asked her flat out, and I was sorry I had. She still didn't say anything. And then she just sort of curled up on the bed. She curled up as tight as a fist and goddamn did she ever cry. Jesus, Jesus, Jesus, B____, I was scared, kind of. I've never seen nothing like that. She didn't make any kind of sound hardly. It was like she was pulling up a rope that was tied to something heavy as the moon. Goddamn, those tears were coming from way, way down. I touched her and every muscle in her was like bowed oak. She was just kind of going uh, uh, uh, her whole body jerking like a heart. Then she threw her arms around me so fast, I thought for a second she wanted to slug me. I couldn't swallow, and I could feel my veins pounding where the inner part of my arm touched her back and shoulders. We held each other so tight, we were like socks rolled up and tucked away in a drawer. I guess I never loved or cared so much about anybody as then.

About, I don't know how long later, she told me about it. We'd went into the kitchen 'cause I was hungry, and she wanted some wine. Her eyes were all puffy and red. Her voice croaked. And every once in a while she'd shiver, and get this scared look in her eye and look all around the room. She was whispering 'cause she didn't want to wake up Max, who's room is right next to the kitchen. But the whispering sort of made it weirder or scarier or something. I kept gulping like some cartoon character, and my feet and hands were like ice. I couldn't look at her.

It was this friend of her ex's who'd did it. She says
they were sitting in her and her old man's living room.
Her old man was at work. He was a medic at Fort
Cartoon. I met him once when he came from Texas,
where he lives now, to see Max. Guy's an extreme
redneck. So anyway, she says she and this guy were
getting high on hash, and just talking about stuff. Anyway, they were just sitting there, getting high, when
just like that, this guy pulls a knife and tells her to strip
and he rapes her. It made me kind of nervous and sick to
hear all that. She told me she'd never told anyone else. I
guess it sounds kind of dumb, but I felt honored that I
was the only person she'd ever told that to. It sort of
made me love her even more. Then just like on some
cop show or something, she started telling me that she
felt all dirty because of what that guy did. It kind of
surprised me that a real woman would talk that way. I
pretty much thought that kind of stuff was just made
up. But she doesn't even watch t.v., except for the news
and tennis matches, so I'm sure she wasn't saying it
because she'd heard someone else say it. But I hugged
her real tight, after she said that, and I told her that
she was the sweetest, most beautiful woman I'd ever
known. I meant it, too. I didn't stop telling her till she
smiled a little.

We went back to the bedroom and got back in bed. I
never did get anything to eat. Pretty soon she was
asleep, but I couldn't sleep at all. It was partly because
of what she'd told me, and partly because of what she'd

made me remember. That's why I'm writing you, B____. I couldn't and I still can't sleep because of what you and me and Stick and Camel saw that one night when we were standing outside the gym. It was the only time the four of us ever just hung out together like that. I don't even know why we were all there together. Do you? I mean, the Stickmeister never hung with the three of us, 'cause we weren't real popular. And Camel could have walked home. Usually it was just you and me who'd be out there, waiting for the activity bus. It was colder than Jennifer Lash's underdrawers out there. Remember? You didn't have a jacket, and you offered five bucks to Camel if he'd let you wear his. I remember we all cracked up when you did that.

So, laying there next to Anna it's like I was reliving that night. I kept seeing the blue car, and how the woman kept saying please, please, please, please, and how she tried to crawl under the car, and how you and me were starting across the street, but Stick grabbed your arm and said, he might have a gun, he might kill her — and then how you just stood there saying Hey! Hey! Hey! And then they were gone. Everything was just taillights all of a sudden. I can't believe we just stood there. And I was so goddamn embarrassed when the cop asked what year the car was, and we didn't know, what the license plate read, and we didn't know. And I think we were all embarrassed when we told the cop our stories. I remember you said she was dressed like a nurse and you saw her on the sidewalk, just walking, and then the car pulled up and the guy pulled her in. Then I told them that, no, no, no, first she tried to crawl under the car, then he pulled her in. Then Camel said no, no, no, there were two guys, and the guy in the passenger seat had a gun. Then Stick said no, no, no, no, I think she was in the car first and tried to get out, and the guy pulled her back in. Come on, guys, Stick said, don't you remember when the guy kept asking her for the keys? And no, Camel, there wasn't a gun. I just thought the guy might have a gun. And I remember, you said, B____, God! What's wrong with you, Stick, that was the woman saying *please*, *please, please*; nobody said a damn thing about no keys! She was crawling under the car and screaming please!

Jesus. Please, keys, tease, ease, bees, knees, cheese. Jeez, what a buncha idiots we must've looked like. But the thing that got me the most, the thing that fucked me up the most that night was when the cop asked the big money, bonus question, what color was the guy? Couldn't tell, you and me said. Too dark. Camel and Stick said, at the same time, black. Then we started arguing. No, no, no, too dark to tell. No, no, no, Afro, he had an Afro. No, butthole, how could you tell? Do you remember if the woman was black? No? Then what makes you think the guy was black? The woman was white, you chump. Yeah? Well what color was her hair? How long was it? How tall was she? Heavyset, was she, or thin? Old or young? Too dark to tell. Too dark to tell. And what makes you think she was in the car first, Stick?

God, what idiots we were. And I sat up in bed that night, after Anna'd told me what she told me, and I couldn't get it out of my head. But I thought about other things, too, B____. I thought about how I used to fantasize when I was a kid, after I'd seen *To Kill a Mockingbird.* I used to fantasize about how I was on trial for raping a white woman, and how I knew I was innocent, and I'd be up on the witness stand with the prosecuting attorney's hot, tomato-faced mug right up in mine. He'd be spitting crap like, Didn'cha, boy? Didn'cha? You lusted afta those white arms, and those pink lips and those pale blue, innocent eyes, didn'cha, nigger boy?

Objection!

Sustained. Mr. Hendershot, I have warned you about —

Forgive me yo honor — and then he dabs his tomato face down with a crumpled hanky — but when ah think of the way these . . . these animals lust afta our sweet belles, why, sir, it makes mah blood boil. No more questions. Yo witness, Mistah Wimply.

And my defender would get up there and sputter and mumble. The prosecutor'd be laughing into his cuffs, dabbing his face, winking and blinking at the jury. Wimply'd look like a fool, but somehow I'd be able to say the right things, and I'd speak as powerfully as Martin Luther King Jr. himself. And while I talked I'd be looking at my accuser with my big puppy eyes and I'd talk about love and justice and peace, equality, never taking my eyes off her beautiful face. She'd start to sweat and tremble, then she'd pass out. The crowd'd go huzzah, hummah, huzzah. The judge would bang away with his gavel. But soon enough the testimony would end, the jury would come back and basically say, hang the black bastud. Then we'd come back the next day, and the judge would say, Scott Winters, you have been found guilty by a jury of your peers. You have committed a vile and foul crime, my boy, and this court has decided to make you pay the ultimate penalty . . . But all of a sudden, B____, my accuser would pop up from her seat and say, No! He's innocent! Innocent, I tell you. I accused him of the crime because I love him, but all he did was ignore me every time I tried to talk to him or smile at him. He ignored me. Then she'd cry like a son of a bitch, and the crowd'd start up with the huzzah, hummah, huzzah. And the judge would be hammering away with his gavel, the prosecutor'd be patting his fat face with his hanky, and the woman would run into my arms. And that'd be that.

Don't ask me why I'd fantasize about that, and I'm not sure if "fantasy" is even the right word. I just played that, whatever it is, in my head, night after night, and I don't know why, exactly, but I think it's because when somebody says rapist, what picture comes to mind? I know I don't have to tell you, B____, it's me and you and your brother and your dad, and my dad, and all our uncles and cousins, and so on. It's like how Anna said at breakfast last year when she was preaching to me like she always does about women's lib stuff. She said,

"Scott, if I were to come back from the doctor's today, came home with tears in my eyes because of what the doctor had told me, what would you say?" Well, I didn't know what she was driving at, and I shrugged and said, "Well, first thing I'd ask is, what'd he tell you?" And she jumped up from her chair and spilled her coffee and mine in the process and said, "Bingo! See! See! 'What did He say' — that's my point. Do you understand me now? We've got these images embedded in our heads and they're based on stereotypes!" I'll tell you what, man, I did get her point, but if I hadn't I woulda said I'd got it just the same. Cripes.

Anyway, there I was in bed with her, listening to her breathing, thinking about those old fantasies, and about that day we saw the woman being snatched off the street, and how this beautiful woman laying next to me had to suffer so hard over something she could never, ever forget. I couldn't sleep. I wanted a cigarette bad, the first time I'd really even thought about squares since her and I moved in together. I slipped out of bed and dressed. I was gonna walk up to the 7-Eleven and buy a pack of Winstons, my old brand. I was gonna walk back home, smoking one after another and think about things like why guys are such dogs, and how in hell Anna could love or trust any guy after what'd happened to her. It was cold that night, and snow was falling, but not too hard or thick. They were big flakes, and the sky was pinkish gray. You could see as far as a block or two. Real beautiful. It was dead quiet, no traffic, no voices, no dogs barking. You know how Colorado Springs can be on a winter night at two in the morning. It's funny, but I kept expecting the night to be split in two by screams, and I imagined myself running to wherever the screams'd come from, and I'd find some bastard pinning a woman down on the sidewalk, holding a blade to her throat, and hissing, shut the fuck up you goddamn cunt. And I'd see his big red balls hanging over her. I'd plow my ol' two-ton mountain boots so hard into them sacks it take a team of surgeons to pull 'em out his stomach. I could see myself taking the knife out his weak hands, and making one clean, quiet slice on his throat, and that'd be that. I'd walk the woman home and call the cops, and split before they got there. I was thinking so deep about this stuff, B____, it took me a while to notice that my fists were clenched, and so were my teeth. And it took me just as long to notice that I was walking, then, in the same goddamn neighborhood where the four of us had seen the woman, the guy, and the blue car.

It really kind of freaked me out. I didn't recognize it right away, because in '69, of course, there'd been a Griff's Burger Bar(f) on that lot. Then they made it into a Taco John's. Now it's some kind of church, but there I was probably standing exactly on the spot where nine years ago that woman'd stood. Man, I just stood there for maybe five minutes. And then I went and sat on the steps of the church. All them things were going through my mind, all the stuff I was fantasizing about, all the stuff I could and couldn't quite remember. Then I started feeling guilty about being there, on my way to get a pack of squares. I hadn't had a cigarette in eight months. Like I said, it was Anna who'd helped me quit them things. It was, in a way, the basis of our relationship. Anna's into health like you wouldn't believe. She used to smoke cigarettes, but quit them and coffee when Max was born. She took up swimming and running to get back in shape after he was six months or so. Then when he was like two or three, she quit eating meat. The first couple times we went out we ate at a pizza place, and it was the first time in my life I'd ever had a pizza with no meat on it. It wasn't bad, but I was still hungry. I told her too, but she said, "It's psychological. You're meat hungry." I paused for a minute and grinned real big. Then she laughed and said, "God, you've got a dirty mind." Well, we went to her place. I'd never even been inside before. It was different, really hippyish. There were plants at every window, and it smelled like incense. There was all this beautiful art on the walls, paintings and prints and lithos. Her bedroom was a loft. It sure didn't look like a welfare house, not what I thought one would look like, anyway. Well, I paid the baby-sitter, even though she didn't want me to. Then we got high. Then we made love.

I'd never felt so good with a woman. It was all so quiet and natural, but still intense. But when I say quiet, I don't mean she was silent. She made so much noise I thought she'd wake her kid. When I say quiet,

though, I mean peaceful, sort of spiritual. She went to
sleep, but I stayed awake, and then I went outside and
lit up a square. When I went back inside, I noticed how
bad I stunk. Tobacco'd never smelled so strong or so
bad to me. I went to the bathroom and washed my
hands and face, tried to brush my teeth with toothpaste
and my finger. Next morning, we got up and she fixed
me a fritata. (Don't know if I spelled that right or not.)
It's this thing with eggs and veggies. We had apple juice
and Morning Thunder tea. At first I thought something was wrong with the juice because it was brown,
but Anna told me it was natural, and was supposed to
look like that. It tasted great. And after breakfast I
didn't have a cigarette, which is what I usually do. It
wasn't hard. I just didn't want one. We went to school,
and met each other during the day as much as we could.
I didn't have a cigarette all day. After classes, I picked
her up and then we got Max from school, and I took
them home. Anna wanted me to stay for dinner, but I
was dying for a smoke. When I got home I smoked like
a fiend. But the more time I spent with her, the less I
cared about cigarettes. It was easy. I quit eating meat,
too. I wasn't whipped, man. It just didn't feel right
anymore.

So, anyway, B____, there I was on the steps of the
church feeling guilty about getting cigarettes. I sat
there for a long time, but then got up and walked back
home. When I got back into bed with Anna, she woke
up, and told me how cold I was. "I went for a walk," I

said, which was true, but it felt like a lie. I felt guilty about a whole lot of things that night — for wanting a cigarette, for being a man, and for not telling her about that night and what we saw. It was a work night, too, even though it felt like a Friday. I knew there'd be hell to pay if I showed up late for work. Old man Van Vordt is a prick-and-a-$^{1}/_{2}$. You show up more than thirty seconds late and he fires you. You cut a piece of lumber as much as a sixteenth of an inch too short and he fires you. You take more than the twenty minutes he gives us for lunch and you might as well pack your trash and ride out of Dodge. In the six months I've worked with him, he's fired about thirty guys. He only wants to tell you something once. Fuck it up, and you die. He pays good money, though, and that's why I keep going back to that freckle-headed ol' fart. Besides, I love the smell of wood, and the precision and beauty of what we do. He's the best cabinetmaker I've ever run into, and for some reason, he likes me. I'm the only black guy he's ever had working for him. Maybe he believes in affirmative action. But anyway, my point is that I decided to stay up that night, 'cause I couldn't sleep, and I didn't want to be late to work. That made me want a cigarette all the more.

I started smoking about five years ago. To tell you the truth I like smoking a lot. Cigarettes, I mean. Pot's OK, but I like the cigarette buzz more, for some reason. And I like the way my lungs fill up. It makes me feel warm inside, makes me dreamy, sort of. I like making smoke rings, french-inhaling, shotguns. And even though it stinks like hell, I like it when my room fills up with smoke. It's like having indoor clouds. I do go through about a can of air freshener a week, and I gotta run fans and keep windows open to kill the smell, but when the sun's shining through my windows in the afternoons, I'll shut 'em, fire up square after square, lay in my bed, and blow cloud after cloud of blue and yellow smoke. And I hate it when a friend busts into my room on those days and says, "Jeezuz, it stinks in here." Hell, I know it stinks, but you can't smell worth a damn if you're inhaling and blowing. And it's my room.

I started smoking in '73, like I say, when I was still living at my folks' place and you were in college at Graceland. I'd went down to Alamosa to visit with Gary T____ and Dale P____. They were juniors, I think, and were living off campus. Let me tell you, if you think those guys were partiers in high school, you shoulda seen 'em then. There whole place was set up for partying. No rugs, black lights, strobe lights, lava lamps. They had a refrigerator in the basement that was filled with beer, maybe twelve cases. They had a wet bar upstairs, and this big-ass cabinet filled with every type of booze you could name. Then there was this fishbowl in the kitchen that was full of joints, pills, and blotter acid. It was unreal. Serious to God, I wasn't into any of that stuff at the time, and most of it I'm still not. I've never done acid, speed, coke, downers, dust, and I can't stand most booze. I might have a beer every so often, but I just nurse the hell out of 'em. Man, I can make a can of beer last for a whole party. Actually, I did speed once in high school, and once again a couple months ago when I was working twelve-hour days at the mill. Anyway, I went up to check out Gary and Dale 'cause I hadn't seen them in a year or more. I was really surprised at what they looked like. Both of 'em had hair down to the middle of their backs. Dale was wearing this big honkin Fu Manchu and Gary had a full beard. It was incredible. Neither of them was playing hoop anymore. Gary'd quit and Dale'd wrecked his knees.

So anyway, they weren't having any party that night, but people kept coming by all afternoon and all night to buy drugs. They had quite a nice business. They were each pulling down about 20 thou a year. It's how they paid their tuition. Far as I know they're still dealing.

So like, we shake hands and bullshit, etc., etc., and they show me around their place, etc., etc., and then Gary's fiancée comes by, and we go down to the basement and sit on beanbags and then Gary brings out a gas mask and a bag of Panama Red. Oh, Lord, I started thinking. What if the cops bust down the door and start blazing away? What if it's bad stuff and we O.D. or something? (Yeah, I was pretty naive.) Then Dale said, "You get high, Scott?" And I said, "Oh sure." So when the mask came my way, I huffed and pulled and sucked, but didn't feel a thing. I took about fifteen hits in all, but still didn't feel a thing. Except I did feel paranoid (or as Gary would say, "noid.") I told 'em I still lived with my folks and they'd kill me if I came home reeking. So Dale reached into his T-shirt pocket and took out a pack of Marlboros, and said, "Smoke these on the way back. You'll smell like cigarettes, and that might make 'em mad, but you won't smell like weed, which'll make 'em toss you out." I put 'em in my pocket, and we hung out for a while longer and talked, etc., etc. Then we ordered a couple pizzas, ate, and then I split back home.

I got back to the Springs about one in the morning and I'd forgot all about the cigarettes till I was almost home, so I pulled off at this junior high parking lot, lit one up. After about five minutes I felt like I was floating. I felt calm. It was weird. I mean, I'd spent the entire evening smoking dope, and hadn't felt a thing, but I was getting ripped on a damn cigarette. Well, that was it, man, I was hooked. Into it big time. My mom was pissed off at me when she found out I was smoking, but what could she say really? I mean, both my folks'd started smoking when they were in their teens, and they smoke maybe a pack a day apiece. Things got a little tense around the house, though, so I moved out.

Like I say, I wanted a cigarette, but I didn't smoke. Anna went to school and I went to work. Things seemed pretty normal. I was dragging ass at work, though, and ol' Van de Man was a demon. "Scott!

Where's those rabbit cuts I asked you for?" "Scott! I
thought I asked you ta clean that planer." "Scott! You
building a goddamn ark or what? Thought I asked you
for them chester drawer legs a half hour ago!" I saw my
career flash before my eyes a half dozen times. It wasn't
only 'cause I was tired, and it wasn't only 'cause I would
have given my left nut for a cigarette, and it wasn't just
that I walked around all with my guts feeling like Jell-O
'cause I was afraid every second of what might happen
to Anna when I wasn't home. It was because I thought
that since she'd told me about the worst thing that'd
ever happened to her, that I should tell her about the
worst thing that I ever let happen to someone else. But
when I got home that afternoon, I made dinner, we ate,
she did the dishes, we went to bed and made love for a
long, long time. And that was it. It took me four hours
to get to sleep that night.

Days went by and days went by and still I didn't say
anything. But all I could think about was how that
woman was trying to dig her nails into the pavement
while she was under that car. And all I could think
about was some bastard holding a knife to my woman's
throat and breaking into her like a bullet. And I started
getting weird and jealous in funny ways, like once
when I drove by campus to pick her up from the library,
and she was out front talking to this dude. She was
standing out on the lawn, holding her books up over her
breasts, and this tall blond bearded dude was craning
over her, smiling, talking, moving his hands like he was

conducting a goddamn band. I could tell they were looking deep in each other's eyes. I thought I could tell she was into this dude. B____, I know this'll sound stupid, but I was sitting there in my car, thinking, you idiot, don't you know what he's got on his mind? Don't you know what he could do to you? I acted like a prick all night long. To her anyway. With Max, I was like Santa Claus. I rode him on my back like a horse, I played checkers with him. I read him a couple stories. Then after everybody was in bed, I slipped out the house, walked to the 7-Eleven, and bought a pack of cigarettes and a bottle of mouthwash. I went to Monument Valley Park and smoked half a pack, washed my mouth, over and over till the bottle was empty, and then I split back home. Soon as I got back I smoked a joint to mask the smell.

I thought we should be getting closer. I thought she should mistrust every man but me. But then I got to thinking that maybe she could sense something about me, knew I was holding something back, which I was. I was holding two things back. I thought she was sensing something, 'cause her attitude was changing at home. She'd gotten pretty rough with Max. Didn't hit him or anything, but she'd go pyro on him if he spilled milk or messed up his clothes. And she only seemed interested in talking to me about stuff she was doing at school. And when all I could say back was something like, ". . . . . ?" she started giving me all this women's lib stuff to read. Gyno-this and eco-gyno-poly-that. And when I still didn't get it, she'd just click her tongue at me and roll her eyes, sigh real loud, and stomp off. She started correcting my English, which is something she'd never done, and she started having long phone conversations with people and she'd never tell me who she was calling. And every time I thought maybe I'd better tell her about what you and me and the fellas saw that night, she'd do something else to piss me off, and I'd keep my mouth shut. I think from the time I lit that first square, the base of our relationship started to crumble. But then she was keeping something from me, too. I didn't know for sure, but I could feel it. I couldn't keep my mind off that tall blond son of a bitch.

I started picking up a pack of smokes on the way to work every day. And I started keeping mouthwash, gum, soap, air freshener, a toothbrush, and deodorant in a day sack in my trunk. Sometimes she'd say to me, "Geez, have you been at work or at a disco?" I'd tell her I just thought she'd like it if I didn't come home smelling like a bear. "You smelled like sawdust," she said, "and I like sawdust." But I couldn't stop smoking. And I started up eating meat again, too. On the way to work, I'd toss my cheese and sprout sandwiches and grab a hoagie, a chilli dog, didn't matter. So I'd play Mr. Tofu Head at home and go to work and let myself get scuzzy as hell. It never occurred to me once to look into other women, but I felt just as guilty. I couldn't sleep for shit, and I was getting kinda soft in bed, if you know what I mean. I couldn't stand myself. And I couldn't stand her. After we'd screw — and it was screwing by then, not love — I couldn't stand the touch of her. It was like every damn day I felt like I was gonna explode. I could see myself dropping to the floor at Anna's feet and begging her to forgive me for all the stuff I was doing, and all the stuff I'd failed to do. I'd beg her to forget that tall motherfucker and come back to me.

B____, I tried and tried and tried to tell her, but I couldn't, and I knew I was smoking a wall between us. I knew that, man, so I'd try every day to quit. I'd crush my cigarettes before leaving work, and flush 'em down the toilet. I'd spray, wash, brush, rinse my ass till I was clean as a pimp. I'd do this every day, and every day I saw them squares, spinning round and round that white water, and going down, I thought that'd be it, that I wouldn't smoke any more. I bought a book on self-hypnosis, and a self-hypnosis tape at this health food place where we used to shop. I tried herbal teas and hot showers, gum, candy, jogging, prayer. And I'd go home every day with a new idea, or a new way of picking up the subject of rape. I figured that of all the reasons I'd gone back to smoking, that was it. One day, I said, "Hey, babe, why don't we start giving money to one of them women's shelter things." She was cooking dinner at the time. It was her day to do it. I was kicking back at the kitchen table, drinking some juice. She didn't say anything for like 30 seconds, enough time for me to get nervous and start looking around. I watched Max tumbling around in the backyard. He looked cute as hell, his hair looked like pure white light the way the sun hit it. Then I looked back at Anna. She just picked up a handful of veggie peelings and flung 'em in the trash. "I think that'd be a good idea," she said, but she was looking really tight, really serious when she said it. I knew something wasn't "organic," as she would say, so I asked her what was up. Well, she flung that red hair out of her face, wiped away some sweat from her forehead with the back of her hand, dried her hands on a towel, and left the room. She came back in a minute with a little stash box, and I was relieved for a second 'cause I thought she was gonna twist up a joint and haul me off to bed. I was smiling, I think. She opened the box, reached in, and tossed a cigarette, my brand, on the table. "I found it in your pocket when I did laundry yesterday," she said. She just stood there. I just sat there. "Busted," I said.

Yeah, we fought about it, but I didn't have too much fight in me, really. What could I say? It was mine. "I trusted you," she said. "You told me that when you met me, quitting smoking was the easiest thing in the world," she said. Scott Winters, I was thinking, a jury of your peers has found you guilty . . . It really surprised me when she started crying. I didn't think she'd took it that serious. I mean, she never'd asked me to quit smoking. Never said a word about it. And it was easy. When we moved in together, I just didn't buy anymore squares. That was it.

From that day on, the day I was busted, is when I

started thinking about getting in touch with you, B____. I wanted to ask you how you felt when Kari found out about you and that chick you were seeing. How you felt when you got busted. Kari called me up one day, after you and she'd split, and she was so angry I could hear the phone lines sizzling. She said, "I just wanna ask you one thing, Scott. Will you be honest with me?" And I said sure I would. And she asked me, "Did B____ really tell you he'd dreamt about me six weeks before he and I actually met? Was that true, Scott?" Well, B____, I'm sorry, bud, but I felt bad for her, and I figured that it wouldn't make any difference since you two'd already split. I told her the truth. I told her, no, you hadn't told me that. Then she asked me if it was true what your girlfriend had told her, that you'd been picked up for flashing back in '72 when you lived in San Francisco, and I told Kari that's what you told me. Then — and her voice got higher and I could tell she was gonna cry — she said, "And then that bitch told me that B____ had gotten a woman pregnant when he was in college. Do you know if that's true?" I told her that I'd heard about it from a very unreliable source. That's all I knew. But it was good enough for her. She started crying, and God did I feel bad. She kept saying, "Thank you, Scott, thank you, thank you. I'm sorry to bother you, but I just wanted the truth for once. All of it. I just wanted to hear someone tell me the truth." She hung up without even saying good-bye.

That's why you haven't heard from me, B____. I

was confused and felt ashamed. In fact, that last letter I got from you a few years back is still unopened. I just figured that Kari had called you up to bust your chops, 'cause of what I'd told her, and you were writing to bust mine. I couldn't take that. And if you don't write back now, I'll understand. Anyway, that time, there at the kitchen table, staring at that cigarette, is when I started thinking about you.

I tried to quit, but I couldn't. Sure, I told her I'd quit again, but I never did. I just got smarter about hiding things. I'd quit smoking close to the end of the workday, always kept my squares in my locker at work. That kind of thing. On weekends, I never even thought about cigarettes. I'd take Max to the playground. I'd go grocery shopping. I'd go down to Pueblo to fish with my folks, with Anna and Max, or by myself, and I'd never even think about them. But I just couldn't do it this time. Anna was OK after a few days, but I could tell things were kind of slipping. And I got to feeling that she didn't care about whether I smoked or not. I knew I had to tell her about that night. I just never could. It's like she could sense what I was gonna say, and she'd say something, or give me a look, and I'd freeze up. Like this one time when she and I took Max to the "Y" for a swim. She and I got out after a few laps and I asked her what that guy might have done if she cried out for help. I'd just kind of blurted it out. I don't think she was ready to talk about this thing at a place like that, at a time like that. She just hugged Max's towel to her chest, and looked at the water. She was quiet so long I didn't think she was gonna say anything. "Well," she said, finally, and her answer was pretty much what I thought it'd be except she didn't say, *You stupid asshole idiot fuck*, but I could feel it — "Scott, he said he would kill me. He probably would have." Then she was quiet for a while, and just slicked her hair back with her hand. Then she said, "There're times I wish he would have." She walked away from me, and dove back into the water. That was it. Right then, I knew I was losing her, and I had to tell her. But you know, sometimes I think if I hadn't tried, I wouldn't be sitting up here on the third floor of Banana Manor, listening to the people next door screw their insides out, and hearing some butthead teenager slamming Fleetwood Mac out his speakers for the world to hear. I wouldn't be sitting inside this stinking little cloud of mine at two, now three, now four in the morning, with a terminal case of writer's cramp, trying to lay down something I wish never'd happened.

I was gonna tell her, B____, about everything, the way we all just stood there and watched a huge piece of that woman's life get sucked away into a car, the make, model, and year of which I guess we'll never know. Man, we watched that piece of her life shrink down to a pair of taillights, and we went on with our own. Yeah, I was gonna tell Anna. I was finally gonna do it, and I was hoping both that she would and wouldn't tell me about that tall blond dude.

I called in sick to work, and ol' Van de Man was pissed because we were behind schedule on a contract we'd had with Pueblo 1st Federal. I'd never took a day off before, though, and I told him that. He pretty much let me slide then, but he did it in Van Vordt style. "You screw me one more time like this, Winters, and ya might as well not come back! Just might as well not come back!" I'm sure that freckled head was hot enough to cook rice. So, anyway, I picked out a great recipe from *Diet for a Small Planet*, and whipped that up. I ran to Weber Street Liquors and bought her a bottle of Mateus rosé. It's her favorite. I was nervous as hell, and couldn't sit down all day. I went to the Safeway twice and bought a pack of Winstons each time. The first one, I opened the pack, drew one, and lit up, but put it out. The next one I opened as soon as I got home, but I crushed 'em into the toilet and flushed. I cleaned up the house and bought flowers. I was so nervous, I was twitching. I paced around the house all afternoon, trying to think up ways I could tell her, but it all sounded so stupid — *More wine, dear? Oh, by the way, I witnessed an abduction of a woman when I was a sophomore in high school, didn't do a damned thing about it, though. It probably led to her rape. Maybe even a murder. Just say when!*" I was thinking, Scott, you dork. What good is a clean house and rosé wine gonna do? I felt like a bozo.

So, I went to pick up Max from school, since I knew it was Anna's day to do the laundry. I took the kid into the backyard and I threw him the football for a while, but I was throwing so hard I just about cracked his ribs. He was OK, though. Didn't even cry all that much, but I hugged him and took him inside, fixed him a snack, and let him watch the tube. I really love that kid, I guess. In a way, I guess. At first I was embarrassed at all the stares him and I used to get when I'd take him places. I'm sure some people thought I'd kidnapped him or something, but after a while I didn't even think about it. I think I know how you must feel about being away from your boy.

Anna came home about a quarter to five. Her eyes were all big and she kept asking what the occasion was, and I kept saying, " 'Cause I love you, that's all." We had dinner, put Max to bed, and broke out the wine. Anna didn't know what was bugging me, but she knew I wasn't very together for some reason or another, and it was like she got nervous, too. She got up after a while and started putting laundry away. I looked at her — from her little pink feet to her bush of red hair — and I was thinking, " 'Cause I love you, that's all." She looked gorgeous, and I just knew that what I was gonna tell her'd bring us closer, even if it started off with some hurt. She started to change the sheets on the bed, but I'd already handled that. I swear, the house never looked cleaner, and she kept asking me why this, and why that, but there wasn't, like, excitement in her voice, but like kind of an almost irritated tone, like she felt bad that she hadn't helped, or that I was trying to tell her how to *really* clean house. She kept getting more and more nervous. I think she was figuring I was gonna propose to her, and she's real nervous about marriage. She says she doesn't even wanna think about marriage till she graduates and gets financially together. You know, just in case the next guy dumps her like the first one did.

So she went back to putting laundry away, and I was following her around the house, just yacking about nothing. Then I just sort of started talking real casual about this essay she'd asked me to read. It was by this woman named Sue Brownmiller. I can't remember the title, and it was pretty tough reading, but it's about how women are better at cooperation and being sensitive than guys, and that's what we need in this world. Maybe that's not all she was saying, but that's basically what I got out of it. Took me forever to read it.

Anyway, I started talking to Anna about the article and she started talking about something we argue about all the time — that if women ran the world, it might be a little bit less organized than it is now, but it would definitely be more peaceful. Instead of saying what I usually say, which is, look, as long as there're men on the planet, there'd still be violence, etc., etc., I figured that here was my chance to get to my point. So I just kind of blurted out, "You know, babe, considering all that's happened to you, I wouldn't be surprised if you hated men." And at first I didn't think she knew what I meant, 'cause she just kept opening up drawers and putting stuff away and closing them back up. I figured she'd just click her tongue at me, and roll her eyes and say, "You missed the point, Scott." But then she kind of turned in my direction, but didn't look at me. She pulled her hair away from her face and flung it back. Then she said, "I'm surprised I don't hate black men. The guy who raped me was black." Then she walked out the room with a stack of laundry in her arms. Then she closed the goddamn door. She closed it soft.

I just stood there, staring at the door, B____. It was like she'd stabbed me in the chest and kicked me in the balls at the same time. I'm not exaggerating, man. My nuts were hurting so bad I had to squat for a minute and take some deep breaths. That ever happen to you, where your blood and adrenaline get pumping so bad it hurts your nuts? It took the wind out of me. It was unreal. I never, ever thought she'd say anything like that to me. It was from Mars, man. Why didn't she tell me that night? I was thinking. Why now, this way, like a weapon? What the fuck did I do to deserve that? I just sat there, and my hands were shaking and I thought for sure I was gonna throw up. I felt sick and dead and I couldn't breathe right. It was like my veins'd been tapped and were leaking out all over the floor.

Then, after my blood slowed a bit, I opened up the drawers she'd just shut and I grabbed 3 or 4 of everything, plus a bunch of shit from the closet. Shoes and things. I packed a couple of bags, and I walked into the living room, and to the front door. I looked around the place. It was damned clean, that's for sure. She saw me from the kitchen and she said, "Where do you think you're going?" I just looked at her and shook my head. I wanted to tell her to stick it, but I just shook my head and stepped out. She was on my heels, though, right dead on my heels. She kept pulling on my shoulder and arm, trying to get me to turn around. She kept saying, "What are you doing? Where are you going? What's going on?" Shit like that. I could see her long blue skirt sweeping around and I could see her pink feet. It was cold out there. I felt bad, B____, bad for all kinds of reasons, but I kept moving, jerking my arm or shoulder away from her, you know? My throat was all clutched up tight, and even if I'd wanted to say something to her I couldn't have. I couldn't look at her either. I stuck my car key into the lock, but before I could twist the lock open she grabbed the key ring, and she was flipping by now, practically screaming, ripping at my wrists and hands with her fingernails. She said, "What's going on? What're you doing? Talk to me, Scott, please," and all that. I grabbed her wrist, forced open her hand, took the keys, got in, cranked it up. I never looked back at her face. If I had, I probably wouldn't've split. I mean she was acting completely innocent, like she didn't have any idea of what she'd said. And for a second there, I wasn't sure I was doing the right thing, or if she'd even understood what she'd said or the way she'd said it. By then I was goddamn crying, too. And as I was backing out, she kept saying please, please, please, Scott, please. That's basically why I'm writing you, brother.

Do you think she knew what she'd done? I mean, here's kind of the reason why, what I'm gonna tell you now.

I tried not to listen, OK, and I was pulling away. I couldn't see good, because of the tears, but I could see her in the rearview mirror. She was standing in the street with her hands in her hair, pulling it back like she does when it's wet. She kept saying please, please, please, Scott, please, but the farther away I got, it started sounding more like keys, keys, keys, Scott, keys.

Right now I don't know, B____. Sometimes you just don't know. Sometimes you just can't tell what you see or hear or feel. Or remember.

                              Take care, man,
                              Love, Scott

Soul Food

/ / / / / /

Look at you. Walking out of that empty post office with the gait of someone who had somewhere to go. Can you see it now? Do you remember? It was the day you acquired the Taste. See the way you walked? Head up, long stride. As though you had someplace to go. As though these are the days and this is the place where anybody has anyplace to go. Get factual, Raymond. Read a book. Three-day beard, filthy corduroys, tape-bound tennis shoes. And what on earth made you smile that wisp of a smile you wore, with those eyebrows leaning into each other, chevron-style? You were trying to look inspired, maybe? Or sure of yourself? What was the effect you were attempting? Why would you do that? Nobody down here in the "Flatlands" cares about you sensitive types. Down here, that's a look that says, "Come and take a chunk of my flesh. Run down to the help kitchen and have them cook it up for you."

Why did you go into the post office in the first place?
Not a dollar for a stamp, not a pencil, not a scrap of
paper on you. The postal guard knew this the moment
you had stepped into the post office. He knew you had
just gone in to get warm. You saw the guard fix his pale,
catfish eyes on you as you moved toward the line. You
neither resisted nor feigned indignance when the guard
stepped up to you, which was wise. He would have cool
cracked your skull without so much as blinking. They
don't hire testy bureaucratic drones in these places anymore. You know that. No pink-pated old men, no
freckle-fingered old women in these places anymore.
No one's going to clear a phlegmy throat and say, "Excuse me, sir. If you're not here to do business, I'm going
to have to ask —" No. A postal guard can kill you if he
or she wants. They're bouncers, assassins, meat hooks
with feet and heads. How lucky you were, Raymond,
when the big man clutched you by the elbow and said,
"If you got money, let me see it." You smiled, as is
proper, but you couldn't help jerking your arm out of
the guard's grip, saying, "It's cold out there, man. What
harm's it do for me to stand in —"

The guard unfastened the loop on his holster, removed his revolver, and pointed its barrel at your chest.
"I ain't got time, nigger," said the guard. You didn't
mind the epithet. You didn't even mind the gun. The
thing that frightened you was the pallidness of the
man's speech, his weary, tiny eyes, the slump of his
shoulders. He would have killed you, Raymond, as

casually as one would switch a television channel. The guard was not angry or territorial or tipsy with power. He was merely doing his job. You left without a word, still smiling.

As you descended the icy post office steps and moved toward the avenue, you held that big head high, kept that back straight. Should I go to Norma's? you wondered, as you stopped at the corner to look for any City Service vehicles. "Service," they call them. Norma, you thought. Then you said to yourself:

No, no, too easy. Too damn easy. Where's the old Phillips pride, man? What's happening to you? 'Sides, you can't go see her no matter how hungry you get. Silly heifer called you all kinds of names . . . and didn't miss a beat. She's got you pegged, bubba, and that's no lie. "Trust you? Love you?" she said, flicking the ash from the tip of her cigarette. "Walk on, fool," she said. "You don't come back here till I get my sixty-one bucks. And since you ain't likely to get it, we ain't likely to see each other for a long time. Get the fuck out before I call my new boy to pick you up by your nose and chuck you out." You left.

Of course she was right. You hadn't seen her in fourteen months, and aren't likely to see her again. You can't be a whore's boy if you can't be monogamous. And you know that if you could come up with sixty-one dollars, you certainly wouldn't give it to her. That kind of money could feed a man as resourceful as yourself for nearly two days. On good, good food, not that soy offal and canned mackerel she used to buy from the state store. Besides this, you never even liked the woman, her sixty-three tattoos, her graphic hair design that read I SWALLOW, her nipple rings. If it weren't for the fact she had money, an apartment, little intelligence, and thought she loved you, you wouldn't have even taken up with her in the first place. The same goes for all the other ones. You know that. You were terrible at boying. If you were unwilling or unable to put your fingers around a fellow's neck because he'd refused to pay, well, you got fired, didn't you? You were fired four times. Before the Failure of '97 you had been a waiter, a shipping and receiving clerk, a stock clerk, a carpet installer, and a purchasing agent at a hotel. You were a collector of underground comics. You grew geraniums on your patio. You fished. You hiked. You painted. You read nineteenth-century novels. You saw Grace on Wednesdays and weekends, and the two of you would watch old sci-fi films. (*Plan Nine from Outer Space* was your favorite.) You would make love, get up at ten, and eat a modest breakfast. You would take her to the zoo, or she would take you to the city theater. You saw *Master Harold and the Boys*. You saw *Blues for Mister Charlie*. You saw *Night of the Iguana*. What could any of this teach you about battering skulls and cheekbones? What did you know of anything more violent than splitting cardboard or shag with a box cutter? You were a terrible whore's boy, and you are only a middling pickpocket.

But these days you like to tell yourself that the Flatlands are less precarious, and certainly more honorable, than life on the Mountain. You're on your own here. There's less to eat, but the food is better. And the "Mountain," that windowless one-hundred-story tangle of concrete, iron, and Plexiglas — fences and walls, electrical ears and eyes, that smothering Leviathan that purrs with the sated lives of bankers, prostitutes, butchers, macemen, lawyers, musicians, teachers, jewelers, whore's boys, plumbers, clergymen, engineers, jackites, physicians, clerks, cab drivers, bureaucrats, and functionaries of every level and stripe — the hive of the only half million people between the Atlantic and the Pacific who can be said to live lives of regularity and peace — sickened you. City Servers on every corner, stingers, batons, pistols at the ready. Helmets. Boots. Knuckles. Those steady hands, gloved and brutal. Those calm voices, unnervingly gracious. *Good afternoon, sir. What is your code? Excuse me, what is your destination? By the way, where is your health card? One moment, sir. When was your last physical? That reminds me: to what whore do you belong? Oh, one more thing. Where is her residence? Gosh, that's odd. What qualifies you for two soy bricks?* But just one wrong word, one moment's hesitation, one vague movement. Just one.

But she paid well. Norma did pay well.

Wrapped as you were in these thoughts, they were poor insulation against that nasty wind. You tried to let them scatter; they were fruitless, you said, dangerous even. You shoved your hands into your pockets and sliced through the throng of people around you. I'm not thinking, you told yourself. Ice popped beneath your feet, broken sidewalk bounced off your toes, skittered away. The world dissolved around you, became invisible, except for the coldness. You tried to take your thoughts to a deeper level, where you couldn't hear them, deep beneath the garbage that day was turning out to be, beneath your thoughts of all the throat biting and eye gouging and nut busting you could not bring yourself to do that day. You felt bad. You sought escape. But where did you think you'd end up?

At the crosswalk, the world seeped into your eyes, nostrils, and ears. The cluster of dazed-looking people around you stood stupid, nondescript. Their ashen faces reminded you of films of Nazi concentration camp prisoners you had seen in school. Those glazed eyes, less than alive, focused inward, as if to scrutinize the soul for the horrid things it might have done, or the penitent things it might have neglected to do, that the body should so utterly suffer. Yet in those same eyes there was a vague surprise, as if they were able, at times, to take an evanescent glimpse at heaven.

Your eyes cut left and right, and you caught glimpses of eyes on you. Those were the ones you need pay no mind; if they were looking, they had nothing. You looked for those who appeared neither inward nor around, but those who looked contented, those who smelled of soap or cigarette smoke, those with clean hands, or sufficient layers of clothing. They were the ones who came down from the Mountain to the Flats to buy drugs or liquor. It struck you as odd that one could find whores only up there in God's country, but all other vicestuffs down here. There you were, thinking again. You almost missed that short, chunky man in an ancient brown wool coat. The man's thick, round head was pinched inside a battered fedora. His eyes jutted, seemingly, everywhere at once. They bulged as if all the air had been sucked from his lungs. There was nothing specific about his appearance that caught your attention. It's never any one thing, is it? It was something general, something organic. He had, as is the street term, "the Taste." He had something; you knew that much. "Sir," you said, "would you happen to have the time?" The man whipped his face toward you. His big eyes, muddy where they should have been brown, yellow where they should have been white, registered all the fear that was appropriate, and then some. But your Serverlike voice, perhaps your greatest asset, hooked him, reeled him in. He who hesitates is duck soup, you thought. The man moved his trembling right hand to his left sleeve before he knew what he was doing. He caught himself, of course, drew back the right hand, put his hands in his pocket, and looked away, tried, in fact, to appear as if he had never heard or seen you. You grinned. The watch would bring good money if it could be smuggled to the Mountain.

The light changed, and his eyes began searching for

an avenue of escape from you. He knew he'd fouled up. He'd probably come down here for brandy, perhaps for sherry. He looked like the type. He'd probably been down here so often that he'd gotten comfortable. But it was clear that he hadn't been here often enough to know one shouldn't grow comfortable. He had the Taste. You were astonished that no one else seemed to notice him.

The gray cluster spilled onto the street. You moved with it, keeping an eye on anyone who stepped too close to you. You tripped, suddenly, falling against the chubby man's arm as if to support yourself. "Sorry, sir," you said, playing it to the bloody end.

"Hey, hey, hey!" said the man. "What're you — hey!" He broke into a shuffling run away from you, his eyes tearing. "Get away from me. Get away. I done nothing to you. I done nothing to you." You watched the man shuffle away, feeling almost sorry for him. But you smiled, then laughed, and said softly to yourself, "Chow time!" No one paid any mind. "Chow time!" you said again, slipping the man's watch into your pocket. Don't even know why I went through all the pretense, you thought. He knew I was after him the second he laid eyes on me. Probably thanking God I didn't take his wallet, and probably doesn't even know he's got no watch. Dumb son of a bitch. Shouldn't have been wearing the goddamn thing in public anyway.

The wind growled and bit your hands and face. Jeez knees, you said. Your thin coat flapped about your loins like insect wings. A flickering of wet snow first darkened the streets, then made them a mottled white. The people faded into the thickening whorls. They looked like ghosts. Nothing to haunt but one another. Nothing to do but eat each other or fade away. Do you remember those days when the world stopped spinning? You could almost hear it, hear it creaking like an old house, thrumming like a far-off storm, then the enormous quiet. There was no madness, no screaming masses filling the streets with their bugging eyes. No erstwhile millionaires leaping from windows. No explosions, no fire, no wailing. Death spread like a slow cool wind. Seeing it, you thought of dust balls under the bed, the imperceptible leak of a tire, the wilt of a flower, a drying lake. Fewer people at the hotel. Fewer people at movies, in bank lines. More of them under bridges, in parks. More hands in your face. Then your job was gone, then your little comics, then Grace, then your apartment, then you remember nothing. Six years of nothing. Two years of construction for a cot and bread. Three years of drug peddling. (You used more than you sold, and your supplier is still looking for you, so far as you know.) Three years of boying. Four years of picking pockets. It's a living, you tell yourself.

People died. Things died. Death in the gleaming, blade-sharp cities. Death in the scrawny hamlets. Little wars blossomed throughout the world like poppies. "Gives people something to do," your friend Michael used to tell you. People, it seemed to him, had done no more than give in to their evolutionary destiny. "Come off that stuff, man," you remember saying to Michael the last time you two spoke. "You're the one giving in, Michael. To the same bullshit despair the Soviet Union gave in to." You felt unsure of yourself. He was older than you, had fought in Viet Nam, had much more education, had been a journalist covering the Gulf War, the War in Europe, the several small and perpetual wars that preceded the breakup of the U.S. Michael had seen things. Michael knew things.

" 'Bullshit despair,' huh? That's good poetry, Ray," he said, "but if you just look at folks, you'll see what I'm saying. The next step is cannibalism, if you ask me. Sure. Go ahead. You can laugh all you want to, but this is what we are, man. This is what we do best: killing, wrecking everything we build. We're wired to grow more savage, not more civilized."

"Uh-oh, now. Check out Professor Mike."

"Jump you, negro. I'm serious."

"That's what scares me."

Neither of you spoke for a while. Static fizzed through the phone line. You considered hanging up and calling back, but were concerned that you might end up with a poorer connection, or no connection at all. One can never tell these days.

"Man, I've seen what folks are like in combat," he said. "No, I'm not just putting it in your face, Ray, but you gotta figure that after being in Southeast Asia, Saudi Arabia, Oman, Kuwait, Holland, France, Grand Rapids, and Duluth — which, by the way, is still smoking like a goddamn landfill — my opinion means something. Folks ain't more than a heartbeat away from cannibalism with every new war. It's the next step in our evolution. . . . I'm serious, Ray. We started as savages and we're gonna end up as savages. I mean, if the universe expands and contracts over aeons, so can human consciousness.

"You think I'd be telling you this if I thought I was the only one it occurred to? That's what my next book's gonna be about. That is, if we can work things out with that publisher in Lagos. Anyway, it's about that next evolutionary step. I've seen it in folks' eyes, Ray. You see how a guy looks after his third or fourth kill. Look, I can't explain it. I thought I could, but I can't. But it's . . . like, like killing's what you gotta do before eating, so . . . Am I making sense? I'm afraid I'm not making sense."

You were going to reply, but really, what could you say? You had seen little violence in your life, avoided it assiduously. When the Union still stood you were too old to draft, after Disunion, all armies were volunteer or vigilante. You moved wherever war was not. What could you say?

"Ray? You hear me, lad? You still listening?"

"Yeah, I'm here." You could tell he was getting excited. He was probably pacing, his bald head gleaming from the exertion, his glasses occasionally sliding down his nose. "After three or four kills?" he said. "Well, a dude gets casual about it. OK, some do, some don't, but some dudes do weird shit, like — like skin and gut and behead . . . like they're butchering a fuckin bull.

After a while, it ain't nothing but meat to some a these guys; just, you know, meat. You see the way they be looking at these kills, man, and it just freezes your guts. They, they just — am I making sense? You get what I'm saying?"

All that you could say was you'd have to think about that, and soon you were speaking of other things: how poor the phone system had become, how long it had been since either of you had heard from this friend or that. He talked about how expensive literary agents had become. You talked about the latest issue of *Eight Ball* you'd read. "Pretty cool," he'd said. He reminisced about what a brave man your father had been, and it made you wonder whether he'd brought your father up because your father fell into the category of all his war buddies who'd skinned, gutted, and beheaded their "kills." You both talked till Mike's wife hollered something about the phone bill. Mike promised to call again, but for some reason he never did. You never spoke again. You were never sure why. There had been no antipathy between you. Perhaps it had to do with the increasingly burdensome exigencies of living — first day to day, and then later, hand to mouth. There was little time for hour-long phone conversations with old friends. And after some time, there was little need for even having friends at all.

You fondled the watch in your pocket, looking for another target, but no one near you had the Taste. One watch wasn't enough, not enough for more than maybe a carton of pigeon eggs, or a half pound of soy cheese, or a can of beans. You looked, you listened. The weak, the stupid, and the gentle. Babies and fools. Those parents who don't turn children out at twelve or thirteen. The Flatland women who don't walk in small weapon-wielding squads. Look for them. Watch for them always. Did you see that man smile? No, he grimaced in pain. Were those women holding hands? No, plainclothes City Server handcuffed to someone. Did you hear children playing around that corner? No, pack of young boys playing kickball with a dog. They would surely kill and eat it after they grew bored with it. You walked on, looking, sniffing. Those who smile too often, or give without apparent ulterior motive; those who do not bribe, connive, steal, double-talk, defraud, extort, conspire; those who listen to or make conversation. The Taste. They have the Taste. You walked round and round, back and forth; perpetual, sharklike movement, bug-eyed, sniffing, looking.

You moved down broken sidewalk, watching the uniformed City Service crew carry away pieces of a bomb-ripped building some terrorist had "stuffed." Their labor was sluggish, indolent. They didn't look like members of the most privileged minority in the country: the employed. But who could blame them? For it was very cold, and their decrepit machinery would break down every so often, and they were forced to lift wheelbarrow loads of shattered brick, glass, sheet rock, and metal into rusty truck beds. They sweated, grunted, slipped on the icy pavement. One worker slipped and fell hard on the ground. She landed on her elbow. The cracking sound made you cringe. You stopped to watch the woman silently writhe on the sidewalk. She strained not to be heard by the fore-worker. No one came to her aid, and finally the fore-worker spotted her. He summoned a vehicle. Two white-jacketed corpsmen walked casually toward the woman; one of them bent over and said something to her. "Go away!" the woman screamed. That smile slid back onto your face. But here it was all right; to smile at such a thing is all right. She hollered, "I'm OK! Leave me to work. Go away. Go away." They heaved her up as she swung at them with her good arm. The other hung at a ninety-degree angle from her body, dangling like a rag doll's. She fought the corpsmen with all she had, but soon enough they strapped her inside the City Service vehicle. One corpsman's sharp backhand shut her up. They drove away. This cracked you up.

The foreworker, who had been standing next to the vehicle, stepped into the office to prepare the termination papers. Already a long line had formed in front of the office. Two large men, all bone and hair, elbowed, then shoved, then slugged each other for first in line. And why not? A Reconstruction job meant an apartment on the Mountain, but access to all that the Flatlands held, too: Ice, Weed, Boy, Girl, Dust, Whiskey, Real Black Market Meats, Tobacco. You knew that in

the time it would take you to walk one block the fore-
worker would be shaking hands with a new employee.
But first in line or last in line would make no difference. Neither would qualifications, nor eagerness to
work. The job would be given to he or she who could
provide an appropriately large enough bribe. You knew
your watch wouldn't buy a minute's work. You kept on.

You turned to look at the growing queue. "Gonna be
one hell of a riot," you whispered. "Maybe I should
come back later to pick up some of the debris." Hunger
wrung your insides, and you very much needed to piss.
No way would you do what a lot of men do: piss on
walls or into gutters out in the open as if marking ter-
ritory. You? You'd go to the Vendor Sector, where there
are still ungated alleys. You cut across the nearly empty
street, and walked as quickly as you could toward the
wide esplanade where the Vendor Sector began. "Best
not move too quick, boy, or you're sure to be followed,"
you said. But it was growing dark, and few would have
seen you. The merchants kept their eyes on their pitiful
ware: old utensils, hand-rolled cigarettes, cast-off
clothing, canned goods, drugs, booze, meat. No one
would have seen you. And as long as you did not
actually step into the sector itself, no City Server would
molest you. You slipped into the alley where merchants
often go to relieve themselves. You kicked through foul
garbage, hid yourself behind a broken piece of plaster
board, undid your pants, and — aahhhh! — made water. The stream cascaded loudly onto a big cardboard

box. "Hope nobody's home," you said. You zipped up your pants, watched the slow steam rise up from the box. Leaving the alley, you kicked through the garbage for a dry cigarette butt. You found, instead, a vial of crack, something that, along with the watch, would bring you a decent meal.

As you stepped onto the esplanade, you heard a noise back in the alley. It was a man's voice, and he was whimpering, begging, moaning. You were only going to watch in hopes of intercepting what you thought was very likely a mugging. You weren't that old. You still had legs that could move. You thought you would crouch behind the boxes, wait till the victim handed over the goods, and go barreling down on the mugger — provided he was alone — throw your shoulder into his belly, and while he lay there stunned, you'd snatch the boon away and bolt out the other end of the alley. A good plan, and you'd done it several times before. So you crouched, peered, focused. They were only twenty yards away, but in the darkness of the alley, you knew they couldn't see you. A tall thin man stood over a thick, roundish figure apparently on his knees. "Gimme it, you fat bastard," the tall one said. And the round one slurred something you could not catch. And then you saw the tall one belt the round one. You heard the report of knuckles striking jawbone or chin. In the same moment the round one yipped like a small dog. You heard him sobbing. "Oh God! I can't. I can't, sir." You heard bone meet bone again. "Gimme that ring, you pig," the tall one said again. In his voice you could almost see his face — pale eyes receded deep behind a jutting brow, pockmarked cheeks, beardless, except for the chin, which held bristly hair as thick and translucent as fishing line, cankered lips that tore and bled a little more with every grimace, lobeless ears, filthy, hoary, cauliflowered. You shivered at this image. You crept closer. Yeah, you thought, Give him the ring. "I ca— I ca— please, sir, I can't. I can't get it off. It don't come off no —" But the tall one's boot pounded the round one's words back down his lungs. You heard the man belch and gasp and cough all at the same time, and you knew he was vomiting bile, food, blood, pulling for air that would not come. You heard the boot again. Then once more. A pause, and then once more. Then you heard the round one's silence. It was the very same sound you heard when the world died. The tall one shoved the round body with a boot, and though you could not make it out, the body, your inner eye watched his dead weight quiver. The tall silhouette reached into his back pocket, and you heard a click, and you saw the millisecond glimmer of a blade. And something burst hot in your belly, deep in your belly. Blood surged through your heart like a torrid gale, and it made your legs weak and your hands tremble.

"I told you, son of a bitch. I told you. I told you. I told you, son of a bitch." The tall one bent over, repeating those words as though they were a prayer. And you saw his elbow pumping back and forth, and you heard, now and then, the knife scrape against the ring, and each time it did your muscles twitched, jittered. "I told you. Didn't I tell you? See, you fuck with me and that's it. Rollo here don't play. He don't play, my man. Rollo don't play." He was whispering, wasn't he? Yes, he was whispering, but you heard him as sharply as if he had spoken into your ear. His fetid breath tickling the hair on your neck. His heat shrinking your skin like a match held too close to cellophane. You heard him grunt, and you heard bone crack. You heard the unmistakable sound of flesh shredding from flesh. You swallowed your scream. Your mind spun. You could no longer see the silhouettes.

When you awoke you were freezing. It was still dark. It had begun snowing again. Far off, you heard the sound of a riot. It was most certainly centered at the construction site, and it reminded you that you had some scavenging to do come early morning. A City Service vehicle droned by the mouth of the alley; police wagon, mail truck, ambulance, snowplow, hearse, all in one, they kept the city safe from every disaster that didn't matter. You stopped to watch the truck till it was well away. Could you move your legs? Yes, you could move your legs, but it hurt. Everything hurt, but that was good. No frostbite.

You dusted the snow from your trousers and your coat and off your hat, and you made your way down the alley. Your feet were numb. Ice had formed on your beard and stung your face. You pulled your collar up, shoved your hands into your coat pockets, felt their contents, removed them. Good. The tall man hadn't seen you, hadn't rifled your clothes. Under the ill light, you tried to read the watch, but you could not. You slipped it back into your pocket. Then, after you found the courage, you looked down upon the naked body of the dead man. Even in that poor light you could see the blood, the missing finger. His wallet lay on his chest. It had not been tossed there, but neatly placed. You could tell. You opened the wallet and came across a three-frame booth photo of the man, his wife, and his children. The son was a handsome, serious-looking boy with dreadlocks. The girl's face was round, rosy, smiling. He was definitely from the Mountain. They were such beautiful people, you thought. Their smiles were so gorgeous that your throat tightened, and the warmest feeling surged through your chest. You thought you would cry, and you waited, held yourself motionless, expecting a great gush of tears. If those tears came, you told yourself, you would fall to your knees and pray to the heavens for forgiveness, pray to the heavens for the deliverance of the world. You hadn't cried in many, many years. You swallowed hard, felt your heart fibrillating, your body trembling. You couldn't breathe or feel or think. You looked at the photos again, hoping that one more look would release the tears. But to your great dismay, and quite nearly to your astonishment, no tears fell at all. So you looked at the body, the poor pitiful man. Perhaps the very same man you yourself had stolen from earlier that day. No tears. No. Quite the contrary. Rather, you began to salivate.

Such sweet flesh. Lips so pink and tender they could be eaten raw. The cheeks so rich with fat they could satiate you for a week. A tongue sandwich with gently sautéed onions. A neck bone stewed for eight hours with fresh tomatoes, scallions, potatoes, carrots, black pepper, and crushed garlic cloves. A brain served on a bed of rice, garnished with parsley straight from the garden. A heart, a liver, a stomach, intestines, and lungs, the stuff of sausages. Steam them, serve them with pasta. Steaks cut from arms, roasts from thighs. You felt lust and horror all in the same moment. Saliva, gushing like springwater. The Taste. And then you did cry. And then you dropped to one knee and retched out long strands of saliva. They lay in dark lines on your corduroys, lay clean as web on your shoes. Look at you. Just look at you.

ABOUT THE AUTHOR

Born in Furstenfeldbruck, Germany, REGINALD McKNIGHT is the son of a career U.S. Air Force noncommissioned officer and served, himself, in the U.S. Marine Corps in the 1970s. After his stint in the military, McKnight earned an associate's degree in anthropology in 1978 and a B.A. in African literature at Colorado College in 1981.

Anne Lennox

He won a Thomas J. Watson Fellowship that took him to West Africa for a year. In 1987 he earned an M.A. in English at the University of Denver with emphasis in creative writing.

McKnight has won several writing awards, including the Bernice M. Slote Award, the Drue Heinz Prize, an O. Henry Award, a Special Citation from the PEN/Hemingway Foundation, a 1991 National Endowment for the Arts grant for literature, a Pushcart Prize, two Kenyon Review Awards for Literary Excellence, and a Whiting Writers' Award in 1995.

His published fiction works include *Moustapha's Eclipse* (1988), a collection, and *I Get on the Bus* (1990), a novel. His nonfiction books include *African American Wisdom* (1994) and *Wisdom of the African World* (1996). He is professor of English in the Creative Writing Program at the University of Maryland in College Park. He is currently at work on a novel tentatively titled *He Sleeps*.